LIANG YUSHENG

Books LLC®, Reference Series, Memphis, USA, 2011. ISBN: 9781156032633. www.booksllc.net. Copyright: http://creativecommons.org/licenses/by-sa/3.0/deed.en

Table of Contents

Adaptations of works by Liang Yusheng
Legend of the White Hair Brides 1
Paladins in Troubled Times 2
Romance of the White Haired Maiden (1999 TV series) 2
Seven Swords 3
Seven Swordsmen 4
Story of the White-haired Demon Girl 5
The Bride with White Hair 6
The Bride with White Hair 2 6
The Patriotic Knights 7
The Romance of the White Hair Maiden (1986 TV series) 7
The Romance of the White Hair Maiden (1995 TV series) 7
White Hair Devil Lady 7

Liang Yusheng
Baifa Monü Zhuan 8
Datang Youxia Zhuan 9

Liang Yusheng 9
Qijian Xia Tianshan 10
Saiwai Qixia Zhuan 12
Xiagu Danxin 13

Liang Yusheng characters
List of Baifa Monü Zhuan characters 13
List of Qijian Xia Tianshan characters 20

Introduction

Purchase of this book entitles you to a free trial membership in the publisher's book club at www.booksllc.net. (Time limited offer.) Simply enter the barcode number from the back cover onto the membership form. The book club entitles you to select from hundreds of thousands of books at no additional charge. You can also download a digital copy of this and related books to read on the go. Simply enter the title or subject onto the search form to find them.

Each chapter in this book ends with a URL to a hyperlinked online version. Type the URL exactly as it appears. If you change the URL's capitalization it won't work. Use the online version to access related pages, websites, footnotes, tables, color photos, updates. Click the version history tab to see the chapter's contributors. Click the edit link to suggest changes.

A large and diverse editor base collaboratively wrote the book, not a single author. After a long process of discussion and debate, the chapters gradually took on a neutral point of view reached through consensus. Additional editors expanded and contributed to chapters striving to achieve balance and comprehensive coverage. This reduced the regional or cultural bias found in many other books and provided access and breadth on subject matter otherwise little documented.

Legend of the White Hair Brides

Legend of the White Hair Brides is a Singaporean television series adapted from Liang Yusheng's novels *Baifa Monü Zhuan*, *Saiwai Qixia Zhuan* and *Qijian Xia Tianshan*. It was first broadcast on TCS-8 in 1996 in Singapore.

Plot

The story is set in the early Qing Dynasty. Zhuo Yihang of the Wudang Sect is in love with Lian Nichang, but Zhuo's fellows strongly oppose their relationship and cause them to break up. Lian is heartbroken and her hair turns white overnight, and she becomes known as the "White Haired Demoness". Zhuo is unwilling to give up his love for Lian and he seeks a rare flower that can turn white hair black again. However, the flower only blooms once every six decades. After a long search, Zhuo finally finds the flower on Mount Heaven, but it is unfortunately destroyed by Zhuo's disciple, Xin Longzi.

Around the same time, Reverend Huiming of the Mount Heaven Sect accepts two boys, Yang Yuncong and Chu Zhaonan, as his students. Several years later, the boys have grown up to become formidable swordsmen. Yang meets Nalan Minghui, the daughter of a Qing general, and falls in love with her after she saved his life once. They secretly conceive a daughter, Yilan Zhu, but can never be together as Nalan's parents have betrothed her to Prince Dodo. Concurrently, "Flying Red Sash" Hamaya, disciple of the White Haired Demoness, also develops a crush on Yang, but Yang rejects her love. Hamaya is heartbroken and her hair turns white overnight, just like her teacher before her. She takes the baby Yilan Zhu away in anger and adopts her as a disciple.

In the meantime, Yang's junior, Chu

Zhaonan, is tempted by fame and wealth, and he betrays his sect to serve the Qing imperial court. More than 20 years later, the grown up Yilan Zhu is unable to escape her fate of following in her predecessors' footsteps, and her hair also turns white. Yang Yuncong and Hamaya meet again on Mount Heaven and they defeat Chu Zhaonan together. Yilan Zhu wants to help her father reconcile with Hamaya, but they refuse and decide to go separate ways.

Cast

- Huang Biren as Lian Nichang
- Lina Ng as Hamaya
- Ann Kok as Nalan Minghui / Yilan Zhu
- Qin Wei as Yang Yuncong
- Shen Huihao as Chu Zhaonan
- Yuan Wenqing as Zhuo Yihang

Source (edited): "http://en.wikipedia.org/wiki/Legend_of_the_White_Hair_Brides"

Paladins in Troubled Times

Paladins in Troubled Times is a 2008 Chinese television series adapted from Liang Yusheng's novel *Datang Youxia Zhuan*. The series was produced by Zhang Jizhong, starring Victor Huang, Shen Xiaohai, TAE, He Zhuoyan, Liu Tianyue and Lu Chen in the lead roles. It was first broadcast on CCTV in 2008.

Plot

The story is set during the Tianbao era during the reign of Emperor Xuanzong during the Tang Dynasty. Dou Lingkan, leader of the Flying Tiger Mountain Sect, and his godson Tie Mole are passing through a small town when they are attracted by a commotion. They realise that Wang Longke, a servant of the warlord An Lushan, is planning to steal a letter from Guo Ziyi's messenger. Apparently, Guo had discovered An Lushan's plans to rebel against the imperial court and he wants to warn the emperor. Tie Mole saves the messenger and becomes involved in the politics of that time. Tie is joined by several righteous pugilists as they attempt to undermine An Lushan's rebellion.

Cast

- Victor Huang as Tie Mole
- Shen Xiaohai as Wang Longke
- TAE as Kongkong'er / Duan Keye
- He Zhuoyan as Wang Yanyu / Shi Hongmei
- Liu Tianyue as Xia Lingshuang
- Lu Chen as Han Zhifen
- Wang Jiusheng as Jingjing'er
- Ba Yin as Yang Mulao / Tie Kunlun / Huangfu Song
- Tong Chun-chung as Emperor Xuanzong of Tang
- Wang Gang as Qin Xiang
- Chen Jiming as Duan Guizhang
- He Sirong as Dou Xianniang
- Tu Men as An Lushan
- Li Zefeng as An Qingxu
- Rocky Hou as An Qingzong
- Yang Niansheng as Han Zhan
- Zhang Baijun as Dou Lingkan
- Wang Jianguo as Guo Ziyi
- Hu Qingshi as Gao Lishi
- Liu Peizhong as Yang Guozhong
- Gao Yuan as Imperial Concubine Yang
- Jiang Hualin as Geshu Han
- Wang Yuzhi as Wang Yanyu's wet nurse
- Ren Baocheng as Du Qianyun
- Zhao Qiang as Zhang Xun
- Chen Panjing as Duan Fei
- Xi Xianfeng as Liu Da
- Zhang Hengping as Blacksmith
- Shi Tongcui as Blacksmith's wife
- Liu Bing as Liu'er
- Li Yuchen as Gou'er
- Zhang Xueying as Hua'er
- Cheng Hongjun as Shi Yiru
- Li Yuan as Mobei Heibao
- Xu Hongzhou as Cui Qianyou
- Song Songlin as Huobo Guiren
- Zhao Shuijin as Li Heng
- Gong Zhixi as Wang Botong
- Tian Yu as Madam Wang
- Tian Haipeng as Opera troupe master

Source (edited): "http://en.wikipedia.org/wiki/Paladins_in_Troubled_Times"

Romance of the White Haired Maiden (1999 TV series)

Romance of the White Haired Maiden is a 1999 Taiwanese television series adapted from Liang Yusheng's novel *Baifa Monü Zhuan*. Alternative Chinese titles for the series are 一代俠女 and 白髮俠女.

Plot

The story begins in the 43rd year of the reign of the Wanli Emperor during the Ming Dynasty. Zhuo Yihang of the Wudang Sect falls in love with the legendary heroine Lian Nichang, disregarding his lover's past feud with his sect.

The treacherous eunuch Wei Zhongxian secretly murders the Taichang Emperor and replaces him with the young Tianqi Emperor, who is effectively a puppet ruler under Wei's control. Wei schemes with the Manchu leader Nurhachi to seize control of Ming China.

Lian Nichang's senior, Murong Chong, is actually a spy working for the Manchus. In order to achieve his ambition of dominating the *Wulin*, he uses a trick to turn Lian and Zhuo Yihang against each other. Lian falsely believes that Zhuo had betrayed her love and her hair turns white overnight. She leaves Zhuo in anger and travels to the remote regions of northern China. Zhuo is unwilling to give up on Lian and he finally resolves his misunderstanding with her after experiencing hardships.

Zhuo and Lian rally a group of pugilists to help them deal with the Manchus invaders. The heroes defeat the Manchu army at Shanhai Pass and temporarily halt the invasion. By then, the Tianqi Emperor had died and is succeeded by the Chongzhen Emperor. Chongzhen believes slanderous rumours and puts general Yuan Chonghuan to death. Without Yuan to defend Shanhai Pass, Zhuo and Lian foresee that Ming China will eventually fall to the Manchus. They decide to permanently retire from the *Jianghu* and lead reclusive lives.

Cast
- Jiang Qinqin as Lian Nichang
- Julian Cheung as Zhuo Yihang
- Lin Fangbing as Red Flower Devil Mother
- Chen Chun-sheng as Murong Chong
- Zhang Heng as Meng Qiuxia
- Ku Pao-ming as Xiao Xiao
- Chang Chin as Miao Huichun
- Chang Luo-chun as Wang Zhaoxi
- Li Hui-ying as Tie Shanhu
- Feng Kuang-jung as Tudou
- Geng Yong as Duniangzi
- Chou Shao-tung as Wei Zhongxian
- Wang Bozhao as Zhu Changluo
- Yu Chia-hui as He E'hua
- Liu Kemian as Geng Shaonan
- Liu Naiyi as Taoist Qingsong

Source (edited): "http://en.wikipedia.org/wiki/Romance_of_the_White_Haired_Maiden_(1999_TV_series)"

Seven Swords

Seven Swords is a 2005 Hong Kong *wuxia* film adapted from Liang Yusheng's novel *Qijian Xia Tianshan*. It was produced and directed by Tsui Hark, and starred Donnie Yen, Leon Lai, Charlie Yeung, Sun Honglei, Lu Yi and Kim So-yeon. It was used as the opening film to the 2005 Venice Film Festival and as a homage to Akira Kurosawa's *Seven Samurai* (1954).

Plot

In the mid-17th century, the Manchus take over sovereignty of China and establish the Qing Dynasty. While nationalistic sentiments start brewing within the martial artists' community (*jianghu*), the Qing government immediately imposes a ban forbidding the common people from practising martial arts. Fire-Wind sees the new law as an opportunity to for himself to make a fortune and offers to help the government execute the new rule. Greedy, cruel and immoral, Fire-Wind ravages northwest China with his army, killing thousands of pugilists as well as innocent civilians. His next goal is to attack Martial Village, which houses a large number of martial artists.

Fu Qingzhu, a retired executioner who served during the previous dynasty, feels an urge to stop Fire-Wind's brutality, and he sets forth to save Martial Village. He brings with him two young villagers, Han Zhibang and Wu Yuanying, to Mount Heaven to seek help from Shadow-Glow, a reclusive master swordsman and sword-forger. Shadow-Glow allows his four students (Chu Zhaonan, Yang Yuncong, Xin Longzi and Mulang) to accompany the trio on their quest. He also gives each of them a special sword he forged, and the seven of them title themselves "Seven Swords". The Seven Swords return to Martial Village in the nick of time and succeed in driving away Fire-Wind's soldiers. In order to buy time for the villagers to prepare for an evacuation, the Seven Swords advance to Fire-Wind's base and cause chaos. During the raid, Chu Zhaonan encounters Fire-Wind's Korean slave girl, Green Pearl, and brings her along as they make their escape.

As the party makes its exodus, strange things start happening along the way. Their food and water supplies are mysteriously poisoned, and their trail is marked by signs leading the enemy to them. The Seven Swords realize that there is a spy among them and understand that they must eliminate him / her before Fire-Wind catches up. Green Pearl immediately becomes a suspect because she does not speak their language. The situation is further complicated by a romantic affair between Chu Zhaonan and Green Pearl. Once, Green Pearl leads Chu into a trap unintentionally and manages to escape despite suffering serious injuries. Chu is captured by Fire-Wind, and Green Pearl manages to inform the other swordsmen before she dies.

The other six swordsmen travel to Fire-Wind's base and engage him in a fierce battle to rescue Chu Zhaonan. During the Swords' absence, the spy, Qiu Dongluo, reveals his identity and begins killing the unsuspecting villagers systematically. He is discovered by the village chief's daughter, Liu Yufang, and eventually killed by her. However, Liu is traumatized by the experience and turns hysterical. Meanwhile, the Seven Swords defeat and slay Fire-Wind, forcing his army to retreat temporarily. The swordsmen return to the hideout, only to find that all the villagers have been killed, except for Liu Yufang and the children. Han Zhibang calms Liu down and decides to stay behind and protect the survivors. The Seven Swords realize that the only way to save the *jianghu* is to persuade the emperor to withdraw the Martial Arts Ban. Liu tells Han that she can take care of the survivors and Han rides away to join his comrades as they travel towards the capital city.

Cast

- Donnie Yen as Chu Zhaonan, wielder of the Dragon
- Leon Lai as Yang Yuncong, wielder of the Transience
- Lau Kar-leung as Fu Qingzhu, wielder of the Unlearnt
- Charlie Yeung as Wu Yuanying, wielder of the Heaven's Fall
- Lu Yi as Han Zhibang, wielder of the Deity
- Duncan Chow as Mulang, wielder of the Celestial Beam
- Tai Li-wu as Xin Longzi, wielder of Star the Chasers
- Sun Honglei as Fire-Wind, a warlord
- Kim So-yeon as Green Pearl, Fire-Wind's Korean slave girl
- Zhang Jingchu as Liu Yufang, Liu Jingyi's daughter and Han Zhibang's

lover
- Ma Jingwu as Shadow-Glow, a reclusive swordsman and sword forger
- Michael Wong as Prince Dokado, a Manchu noble
- Jason Pai as Liu Jingyi, the village chief
- Chik Koon-kwan as Qiu Dongluo, the traitor
- Huang Peng as Guan Sandao, a villager
- Zhang Chao as Zhang Huazhao, a villager
- Chen Jiajia as Kualo, Fire-Wind's follower
- Liu Mingzhe as Jiaoci, Fire-Wind's follower
- Li Haitao as Siyilang, Fire-Wind's follower
- Jiang Guangjin as Sanzi, Fire-Wind's follower
- Xie Zhang as Bald Lion, Fire-Wind's follower
- Wang Chi-man as Dagger Peak, Fire-Wind's follower
- Zhang Jie as Hair Wolf, Fire-Wind's follower
- Tang Tengfei as Stone Beast, Fire-Wind's follower
- Liu Zhenbao as Mud Trot, Fire-Wind's follower
- Lin Haibin as Sangen, Fire-Wind's follower
- Guo Fengqiang as Black Spirit, Fire-Wind's follower
- Jia Kun as Bangmuzi, Fire-Wind's follower

Production

The film, the first of a planned six part film franchise, was approximately four hours long, but was cut to 153 minutes.

Sequel

Tsui Hark intended *Seven Swords* to be a hexalogy, however the prospects for the second installment have not come to fruition. In 2008, Tsui was known to be still developing the script for the sequel in between production and/or direction of other projects; the actual release and production for the sequel had yet to officially be announced. It is believed that Tsui is completing scripts for both the second and third installments of the film to complete the hexalogy in successive development and production.

As of 2011, there has been no news of *Seven Swords* at all, and there is speculation that it would not be completed as planned. The last known news about the film was in its pre-production phase between 2007-2008, yet neither Tsui Hark nor anyone attached to the film made any statement of commitment to the planned hexalogy for about 3-4 years. While unconfirmed, it is believed the film has been stalled or quietly scrapped due to lack of interest in completing the story.

Source (edited): "http://en.wikipedia.org/wiki/Seven_Swords"

Seven Swordsmen

Seven Swordsmen is a 2006 Hong Kong and mainland China co-produced television series directed by Clarence Fok and produced by Tsui Hark. The series is adapted from Liang Yusheng's novels *Qijian Xia Tianshan* and *Saiwai Qixia Zhuan*. It is also the derived counterpart of the 2005 film *Seven Swords*, which was also directed and produced by Tsui Hark.

Plot

In 1664, the Manchus seize control of China and establish the Qing Dynasty. The Qing government issues a martial arts ban, forbidding the common people from practising martial arts and possessing weapons. Prince Dokado, a Manchu noble, leads an army to eliminate those who defy the order. Dokado's men kill many pugilists before assaulting Martial Village, which houses rebels from the Red Spears Society, an anti-Qing secret organization. Two young villagers, Han Zhibang and Wu Yuanying, break out of the siege and follow Fu Qingzhu to Mount Heaven to seek help from Master Huiming, a reclusive martial artist and sword forger.

Huiming allows his four students (Chu Zhaonan, Yang Yuncong, Xin Longzi and Mulang) to join the trio on their heroic quest to save the *wulin* (martial artists' community) from the Qing government's persecution. Each of the seven men receives a special sword from Huiming, and they title themselves "Seven Swords".

The Seven Swords return in the nick of time and save the villagers from attacking Qing soldiers. However, they decide to split up temporarily later to avoid trouble, and embark on their respective missions and adventures. Han Zhibang and Mulang remain with the villagers, while Fu Qingzhu, Xin Longzi and Wu Yuanying travel to the capital city to assassinate the Qing ruler.

Meanwhile, Chu Zhaonan falls into a trap and is captured by the Qing general Fenghuo Liancheng. Chu falls in love with Fenghuo Liancheng's slave girl, Lüzhu, but the romance ends in tragedy, as Lüzhu sacrifices her life to help him escape. Chu meets Yang Yuncong in northwestern China and they join the Desert Eagles, a tribal anti-Qing organization led by the legendary heroine, Feihongjin. Yang is wounded during a battle with Qing forces, and is rescued by Nalan Minghui, an enemy general's daughter. They fall in love, despite standing on opposing sides, but are not fated to be together, as Nalan is engaged to Dokado. However, Nalan is already pregnant with Yang's child and she gives birth to a baby girl later.

In the capital city, Fu Qingzhu and company sneak into the palace and attempt to assassinate the Shunzhi Emperor, but ironically, they save the emperor from a coup staged by some nobles instead. In Hangzhou, Han Zhibang is elected as the new leader of the Red Spears Society for his heroic acts in rescuing his imprisoned comrades. After the reunion of the Seven Swords, Chu Zhaonan pretends to defect to the enemy and use the opportunity to get close to Dokado and assassinate him. Chu's plan fails, as Dokado is aware of his intention, and manipulates him into killing some of the rebels, causing Chu's fellows to start doubting his loyalty.

Eventually, to prove his innocence, Chu and the other six swordsmen challenge Dokado to a battle on the Qiantang River bank. Although the battle concludes with Dokado's defeat, it also causes the division of the Seven Swords. Yang Yuncong is killed in action; Xin Longzi goes missing after entering a fit of insanity; Mulang returns to Mount Heaven in shame with Yang's infant daughter after causing a major blunder by allowing the enemy to infiltrate the rebels' hideout; Chu is morally weakened after the mentally devastating experiences he went through, and he abandons his fellows along with his conscience. Fu Qingzhu and Wu Yuanying embark on a search for their missing comrades, while Han Zhibang stays behind to help the surviving rebels rebuild their force.

Cast

- Vincent Zhao as Chu Zhaonan (楚昭南), wielder of the Dragon (由龍)
- Wang Xuebing as Yang Yuncong (楊雲驄), wielder of the Transience (青干)
- Ji Chunhua as Xin Longzi (辛龍子), wielder of the Star Chasers (競星)
- Qiao Zhenyu as Mulang (穆郎), wielder of the Sun and Moon (日月)
- Zhang Bo as Han Zhibang (韓志邦), wielder of the Deity (舍神)
- Sang Weilin as Wu Yuanying (武元英), wielder of the Heaven's Fall (天瀑)
- Yu Chenghui as Fu Qingzhu (傅青主), wielder of Unlearnt (莫問)
- Ray Lui as Dokado (多格多), a Manchu prince and primary antagonist of the series
- Ada Choi as Feihongjin (飛紅巾; Flying Red Sash), leader of the Desert Eagles
- Li Xiaoran as Nalan Minghui (納蘭明慧), Nalan Xiuji's daughter and Yang Yuncong's lover
- Wang Likun as Liu Yufang (劉郁芳), Liu Jingyi's daughter
- Bryan Leung as Liu Jingyi (劉精一), chief of Martial Village
- Askar as Ai'erjiang (艾爾江), a singer and Feihongjin's ex-lover
- Sun Feifei as Dong Xiaowan (董小宛), Mao Pijiang's wife who was forced to be Shunzhi's concubine
- Edell Ai as Lüzhu (綠珠; Green Pearl), a slave girl who becomes Chu Zhaonan's first love
- Eryang as Nalan Xiuji (納蘭秀吉), a Manchu general
- Xu Xiangdong as Niuhuru (紐祜魯), Dokado's teacher
- Sun Jiankui AS Qi Zhenjun (齊真君), a swordsman hired by Dokado to fight the Seven Swords
- Tan Kai as Fenghuo Liancheng (風火連城; Fire Wind), Manchu general and former *baturu*
- Gao Lu as Chuntao (春桃), Nalan Minghui's servant
- Xie Zhenwei as the Shunzhi Emperor (順治皇帝), ruler of the Qing Empire
- Dai Chunrong as Empress Dowager Xiaozhuang (孝莊皇太后), Shunzhi's mother
- Guo Hongjie as Zhang Chengbin (張承斌), Dokado's deputy
- Liu Tieyong as Zhang Kui (張魁), Dokado's deputy
- Zhang Xin as Qiu Dongluo (邱東洛), traitor of Martial Village
- Wang Huarong as Zhang Huazhao (張華昭), the oldest of Martial Village's children
- Ma Ji as Gu Sandao (顧三刀), a villager
- Chen Zhou as Zhang Laifu (張來福), a villager
- Zheng Li as Zhou Chaotai (周朝泰), a villager
- Zhou He as Shao Zhanpeng (邵展鵬), a villager
- Milading as Ailike (埃里克), Feihongjin's deputy
- Dili Reba'ao as Manlingna (曼玲娜), Kelimu's wife
- Ma Jingwu as Master Huiming (晦明大師; Master Shadow Glow), a reclusive swordsman and sword forger
- Zhu Feng as Mao Pijiang (冒辟疆), Dong Xiaowan's husband
- Wang Xinfen as the White Haired Demoness (白髮魔女), teacher of Feihongjin and ex-lover of Master Huiming

Source (edited): "http://en.wikipedia.org/wiki/Seven_Swordsmen"

Story of the White-haired Demon Girl

Story of the White-haired Demon Girl is a three-part 1959 Hong Kong *wuxia* film adapted from Liang Yusheng's novel *Baifa Monü Zhuan*. The film was directed by Lee Fa and starred Law Yim-hing and Cheung Ying.

Cast

- Law Yim-hing as Lin Ngai-seung
- Cheung Ying as Cheuk Yat-hong
- Lin Chiao
- Sze-ma Wah-lung
- Wong Chor-san
- Lee Yuet-ching
- Shih Kien
- Siu Hon-sang
- Lee Heung-kam
- Law Lan
- Lau Kar-leung
- Tang Chia

Source (edited): "http://en.wikipedia.org/wiki/Story_of_the_White-haired_Demon_Girl"

The Bride with White Hair

The Bride with White Hair is a 1993 Hong Kong *wuxia*-romance film directed by Ronny Yu and starring Brigitte Lin and Leslie Cheung.

The film's main character, Lian Nichang, is loosely based on the protagonist of Liang Yusheng's novel *Baifa Monü Zhuan*, which had earlier served as source material for the 1982 film *Wolf Devil Woman*. However, Yu saw the film as a Romeo and Juliet story and said that the lovers' struggle against fate and their heroic duty inspired him more than the familiar trappings of most martial arts adventure films. As such, the film departs significantly from the original source.

A sequel, *The Bride with White Hair 2*, directed by David Wu, was released later in the same year.

Plot

Zhuo Yihang was raised by Taoist Ziyang of the Wudang Sect and groomed to become a young chivalrous swordsman. He is placed in command of a coalition army formed by the eight major martial arts sects, which aims to prevent an evil cult from infiltrating China. During a battle against the cult, Zhuo meets a young woman called Lian Nichang and falls in love with her. She was an orphan, and was raised by wolves as an infant before being adopted by Ji Wushuang, the Siamese twins who lead the cult. After consummating their romance, Lian decides to leave the cult and follow Zhuo in pursuit of an ordinary life away from the *Jianghu* (martial arts community).

Lian succeeds in leaving the cult after suffering great pains. Meanwhile, Zhuo returns to Wudang and is horrified to see that his fellows have been murdered. The coalition believes that Lian is responsible and attack her when he arrives to meet Zhuo. Zhuo is forced to turn against Lian, and she morphs into a vicious white-haired killer after feeling that Zhuo had betrayed her love. In anger, Lian kills all the coalition members present. Suddenly, Ji Wushuang appears and reveals that he/she is actually the one who killed the Wudang people. Zhuo and Lian combine their strength to defeat and kill Ji. However, even after the victory, Lian vows never to forgive Zhuo for betraying her and walks away with Zhuo looking on helplessly.

Cast

- Brigitte Lin as Lian Nichang
- Leslie Cheung as Zhuo Yihang
  - Leila Tong as young Zhuo Yihang
- Francis Ng as male Ji Wushuang
- Elaine Lui as female Ji Wushuang
- Yammie Lam as He Lühua
- Joseph Cheng as Yu Xincheng
- Eddy Ko as Wu Sangui
- Law Lok-lam as Taoist Baiyun
- Pau Fung as Taoist Ziyang
- Jeffrey Lau as sect elder
- Wong Gwan-hong
- Sam Hoh
- Chang Kin-ming

Source (edited): "http://en.wikipedia.org/wiki/The_Bride_with_White_Hair"

The Bride with White Hair 2

The Bride with White Hair 2 is a 1993 Hong Kong *wuxia*-romance film directed by David Wu. It is the sequel to *The Bride with White Hair*, with Brigitte Lin and Leslie Cheung reprising their roles as Lian Nichang and Zhuo Yihang. Although the first film is based on Liang Yusheng's *Baifa Monü Zhuan*, this film is almost independent of the novel except for the main characters' names.

Plot

Lian Nichang felt betrayed by her lover, Zhuo Yihang, and has since morphed into the vicious White-haired Witch. She builds a feminist cult that accepts women who were exploited by men. Its members include Chen Yuanyuan, who was betrayed by Wu Sangui. Meanwhile, Zhuo awaits on a snow-capped mountain for a rare flower to bloom, as he believes that it can turn Lian's hair black again. Lian vows to kill the surviving members of the eight major martial arts sects, who view her as their sworn enemy after she killed their seniors.

Feng Junjie, heir to the Wudang Sect's leadership position, marries Yu Qin with the elders of the other sects as the matchmakers. On the wedding night, Lian appears and kidnaps Yu, leaving behind a trail of destruction and corpses. Feng survives the massacre and plans with the survivors to infiltrate the Witch's base and rescue his wife. Meanwhile, Lian brainwashes Yu through a series of rituals and makes her see her husband and the eight sects as foes.

Feng and his companions confront the Witch and her followers in a battle but are defeated and only Feng and his friend are left of the group. They travel to the mountain in search of Zhuo Yihang, who is the only person that can prevent the Witch from continuing with her brutal massacres. After enduring hardship, they did not find Zhuo and decide to return to the Witch's base in a final attempt to save Yu Qin. Feng is no match for Lian and is almost killed by her when Zhuo suddenly appears and stops her.

Lian uses her hair to pierce through Zhuo's body, critically wounding him, but she refrains from killing him as her hatred towards him gradually subsides. Just then, Chen Yuanyuan stabs Lian for betraying the cult's founding principles, causing Lian to pull her hair out from Zhuo's body. The film ends with the deaths of Zhuo and Lian, who finally forget their past feud and are laid to rest together as lovers. On the other hand, Feng is reunited with his wife, who has recovered from her trance.

Cast
- Brigitte Lin as Lian Nichang
- Leslie Cheung as Zhuo Yihang
- Christy Chung as Ling Yue'er
- Sunny Chan as Feng Junjie
- Joey Meng as Yu Qin
- Cheung Kwok-leung as Duan Qi
- Lily Chung as Xinghui
- Lee Heung-kam as Emei Granny
- Ruth Winona Tao as Chen Yuanyuan
- Eddy Ko as Wu Sangui
- Law Lan as sect elder
- Yu Chun-fung as Lan Lang
- Richard Suen as Lühen
- Jacky Yeung as Yi Fengxing
- Wong Sun as sect elder
- Yeung Jing-jing
- Lee Wai-choh

Source (edited): "http://en.wikipedia.org/wiki/The_Bride_with_White_Hair_2"

The Patriotic Knights

The Patriotic Knights is a 2006 Chinese television series adapted from Liang Yusheng's *wuxia* novel *Xiagu Danxin*. The series starred Chen Long, Stephanie Hsiao, Wallace Chung and He Meitian in the lead roles. Production companies Zhejiang HG Entertainment Co., Ltd. and Jiangsu Broadcast & Television Group invested a total of 25,000,000 yuan in the project.

Cast
- Chen Long as Jin Zhuliu
- Stephanie Hsiao as Shi Hongying
- Wallace Chung as Li Nanxing
- He Meitian as Zhong Yanyan (Gongsun Yan)
- Jing Gangshan as Jin Shiyi
- Niu Mengmeng as Li Shengnan
- Eddy Ko as Jiang Haitian
- Shen Junyi as Shi Baidu
- Jewel Lee as He Daniang
- Norman Chu as Meng Shentong
- Chen Zhihui as Yuan Hai
- He Jiayi

Source (edited): "http://en.wikipedia.org/wiki/The_Patriotic_Knights"

The Romance of the White Hair Maiden (1986 TV series)

The Romance of the White Hair Maiden is a Hong Kong television series adapted from Liang Yusheng's novel *Baifa Monü Zhuan*. The series was first broadcast on ATV in Hong Kong in 1986.

Cast
- Bonnie Ngai as Lin Ngai-seung
- Savio Tsang as Cheuk Yat-hong
- Chen Kuan-tai as Ngok Ming-or
- Wong Jo-see as Tit San-wu
- Amy Yip as Mang Chau-ha
- Cheng Lui as Kam Tuk-yee
- Lau Wan-fung as Shek Ho
- Cheung Kam as Pak Man
- Lau Siu-kwan as Kang Siu-nam
- Kam Tung as Ngai Chung-yin
- Willie Lau as Muk-yung Chung
- Cheung Tsang as Tit Fei-lung
- So Suk-ping as Muk Kau-neung
- Tong Pan-cheung as Wong Chiu-hei
- Cho Tat-wah as Taoist Pak-shek
- Pau Hon-lam as Cheuk Chung-lin
- Tam Nga-tik as Wan Hing-pong
- Leung Ming as Hung Ting-bat
- Lai Suen as Red Flower Devil Mother
- Au Wing-hon as Chu Seung-lok
- Ng Tsi-yin as Ho Ngok-wah
- Ling Man-hoi as Yuen Sung-wan
- Lee Ka-ling as Hak Ping-ting
- Ting Ying as Madam Hak
- Wong Wai as Chu Yau-hau

Source (edited): "http://en.wikipedia.org/wiki/The_Romance_of_the_White_Hair_Maiden_(1986_TV_series)"

The Romance of the White Hair Maiden (1995 TV series)

The Romance of the White Hair Maiden is a Hong Kong television series adapted from Liang Yusheng's novel *Baifa Monü Zhuan*. The series was first broadcast on TVB in Hong Kong in 1995.

Cast
- Ada Choi as Lin Ngai-seung
- Timmy Ho as Cheuk Yat-hong
- Gary Chan as Ngok Ming-or
- Chow Ching as Ho Ngok-wah
- Wong Wai as Ngai Chung-yin
- Newton Lai as Lei Tsi-sing
- Joanna Chan as Tit San-wu
- Jason Pai as Tit Fei-lung
- Wu Yuet-san as Wong Chiu-hei
- Joe Ma as Chu Seung-lok
- Zhang Yan as Mang Chau-ha
- Ma Hoi-lun as Red Flower Devil Mother
- Chun Wong as Yuen Bat-kwai
- Lo Mang as Fok Tin-to
- Lee Kwai-ying as Ling Muk-wah
- Henry Lee as Taoist Pak-shek
- Kwan Ching as Kam Tuk-yee

Source (edited): "http://en.wikipedia.org/wiki/The_Romance_of_the_White_Hair_Maiden_(1995_TV_series)"

White Hair Devil Lady

White Hair Devil Lady, alternatively known as *Sorceress' Wrath*, is a 1980 Hong Kong *wuxia* film adapted from

Liang Yusheng's novel *Baifa Monü Zhuan*. The film was directed by Chang Hsin-yen and starred Paw Hee-ching and Henry Fong.

Cast

- Paw Hee-ching as Lin Ngai-seung
- Henry Fong as Cheuk Yat-hong
- Leanne Liu as Tit San-wu
- Chiang Han as Muk-yung Chung
- Ping Fan as Tit Fei-lung
- Cheung Ping as Ngok Ming-or
- Mo Yau-ming
- Wong Yeung
- Lau Wan-fung
- Leung Hang
- Leung Hang
- Hau Pui-man
- Chan Tsung
- Tsui Lik
- Lam Tit-ching
- Chan Kwok-kuen
- Chik Ngai-hung

Source (edited): "http://en.wikipedia.org/wiki/White_Hair_Devil_Lady"

Baifa Monü Zhuan

Baifa Monü Zhuan is a *wuxia* novel serialized by Liang Yusheng between August 5, 1957 and September 8, 1958. It is closely related to *Qijian Xia Tianshan* and *Saiwai Qixia Zhuan*. The novel has been adapted into films and television series, such as *The Bride with White Hair* and *The Romance of the White Hair Maiden*.

Plot

The story begins in the Ming Dynasty during the later reign of the Wanli Emperor. Lian Nichang, a female bandit leader nicknamed "Jade Rakshasa", is introduced as an impressive vigilante-heroine who uses her legendary swordplay skills to uphold justice and punish the wicked. Meanwhile, many government officials are implicated in a scandal to depose the crown prince, and they are executed or imprisoned. Zhuo Yihang of the Wudang Sect helps the crown prince reveal the truth behind the case and succeeds in clearing the name of his father, who was wrongly put to death.

While on his journey home, Zhuo passes by Mount Hua, where he meets a beautiful young maiden and falls in love with her. The following night, Zhuo joins some pugilists in a duel against the "Jade Rakshasa". However, Zhuo is shocked when he sees that the woman he met earlier is actually the Jade Rakshasa. He makes another startling discovery that the pugilists he is helping are actually spies working for the Manchus. Zhuo switches sides and helps Lian Nichang defeat the enemy. They meet a formidable swordsman named Yue Mingke, who is a military attaché serving under Xiong Tingbi.

After a duel, Yue and Lian realize that their respective teachers used to be a loving couple, but have separated due to a rivalry over achieving supremacy in swordplay.

In the meantime, the Taichang Emperor dies after consuming the mysterious Red Pills and is succeeded by the young Tianqi Emperor. The eunuch Wei Zhongxian and the emperor's wet nurse Madam Ke use the opportunity to deceive the naive ruler and usurp state power. Wei forms his own political clique and starts persecuting his opponents and the loyalists to consolidate power. Lian Nichang, Zhuo Yihang and Yue Mingke side with the loyalists and oppose Wei Zhongxian, playing key roles in disrupting Wei's evil plans in their respective adventures.

At one point, Yue Mingke is devastated after his lover, Tie Shanhu, dies tragically at the hands of Wei Zhongxian's lackeys. He becomes disillusioned with human society and becomes a monk, renaming himself "Reverend Huiming". He settles in the Mount Heaven region and spends his time studying martial arts.

During that time, Zhuo and Lian start to develop a romance and Zhuo is poised to become the new leader of the Wudang Sect. However, as Lian has a history of bad blood with Wudang, Zhuo's seniors and fellows strongly oppose his relationship with Lian. During a fight between Lian and Wudang's elders, Zhuo accidentally attacks Lian, causing her to misunderstand that he has betrayed her love. Lian is heartbroken and her hair turns white after she awakes from a long sleep. Depressed by her new looks, she travels to Mount Heaven and leads a reclusive life there.

Years later, Lian Nichang makes her name in the Mount Heaven region by slaying villains and defeating expert pugilists. She is known to the locals as the "White Haired Demoness". Meanwhile, Zhuo Yihang suffers from an emotional breakdown after losing Lian, and he leaves the Wudang Sect in search of his lover. After a long journey, Zhuo finally meets Lian on Mount Heaven, but she remains cold and indifferent towards him, refusing to accept his apologies. Zhuo learns that there is a rare flower that can turn white hair black again, but the flower only blooms once every six decades. He finds it and waits, hoping that it will bloom one day and allow him to reunite with Lian Nichang.

Characters

- Lian Nichang (練霓裳) - nicknamed "Jade Rakshasa" (玉羅刹). She was raised by wolves as an infant and later adopted and tutored by Ling Muhua. Her prowess in swordplay and *qinggong* is legendary, and she uses her skills to deliver justice like a vigilante. Though beautiful in appearance, she is deadly, as her sword movements are extremely brutal and aggressive. She also metes out draconian punishments and torturous deaths to her enemies, causing her to be seen as a menacing demoness in the *jianghu*. She becomes known as the "White Haired Demoness" (白髮魔女) after her hair turns white.
- Zhuo Yihang (卓一航) - son of Zhuo Jixian. He comes from a family of scholars and grows up to become a

cultured and refined gentleman. He learns swordplay from Taoist Ziyang and later succeeds the latter as leader of the Wudang Sect.
- Yue Mingke (岳鳴珂) – a military attaché serving under Xiong Tingbi. He was tutored in martial arts by Huo Tiandu and becomes a formidable swordsman. He joins the protagonists in opposing Wei Zhongxian, and becomes a fugitive after Xiong is wrongly put to death. He becomes disillusioned with human society after witnessing the tragic death of Tie Shanhu and becomes a monk, renaming himself "Reverend Huiming" (晦明禪師). He travels to Mount Heaven and settles there, spending his time studying martial arts.

Source (edited): "http://en.wikipedia.org/wiki/Baifa_Mon%C3%BC_Zhuan"

Datang Youxia Zhuan

Datang Youxia Zhuan is a *wuxia* novel by Liang Yusheng. It was written between January 1, 1963 and June 14, 1964. The novel is the first part of a trilogy, and is followed by *Longfeng Baocha Yuan* and *Huijian Xinmo*.

Plot
The story is set in the Tianbao era of the Tang Dynasty during the reign of Emperor Xuanzong. The emperor appoints the incompetent Yang Guozhong as chancellor out of nepotism because Yang's cousin, Yang Yuhuan, is the emperor's favourite concubine. The Tang government gradually sinks into corruption under Yang's ineffective leadership and Yang's supporters dominate the political arena. The power hungry barbarian An Lushan wins the emperor's trust through flattery and the emperor promotes him to the rank of *jiedushi* of Fanyang. An wields great military power in his hands and secretly builds up his forces in preparation for a rebellion.

In the *jianghu*, the bandit lords Dou Lingkan and Wang Botong compete fiercely with each other for the position of chief of the *wulin* (martial artists' community). Dou and his brothers have the support of Duan Guizhang, a renowned swordsman who is also Dou's brother-in-law. On the other hand, Wang cooperates with An Lushan to achieve his goal, while recruiting several pugilists to serve him and sending his children to be tutored by martial arts exponents.

Duan Guizhang maintains a close friendship with a former government official called Shi Yiru. Their wives give birth to a boy called Duan Keye and a girl named Shi Ruomei respectively. An Lushan sends his men to bring Duan to meet him but Duan was not in then, so Shi went in place of him. Shi is held hostage in An's residence and Duan and Dou Lingkan's godson, Tie Mole, go to rescue him. They fail and Shi dies while Duan is severely wounded. They are saved from An's men by Nan Jiyun and Huangfu Song.

Kongkong'er, one of Wang Botong's lackeys, shows up and steals the baby Duan Keye, in order to force Duan Guizhang not to side with Dou Lingkan. Subsequently, Dou is slain by Wang's daughter, Wang Yanyu, in a fight and loses his title of chief of the *wulin*. Tie Mole escapes amidst the chaos with Nan Jiyun's help and vows to avenge his godfather. Duan Guizhang sends Tie to learn martial arts from a reclusive master. Seven years later when Tie has achieved a certain level of prowess in his skills, he returns to civilisation, only to find himself stranded in the chaotic situation of the An Shi Rebellion.

Tie Mole has a series of adventures, including undermining An Lushan's rebellion force by capturing Wang Botong's mountain stronghold and exposing the truth behind a 20-year old mystery and clearing Huangfu Song's name. Tie finds himself entangled in a complex love triangle with Wang Yanyu and another maiden called Han Zhifen. He saves the emperor and flees with the imperial forces after the capital cities Luoyang and Chang'an fell to An Lushan's rebel forces. He is also involved in the historical incident at Mawei courier station, when the discontented soldiers killed Yang Guozhong and demanded that the emperor put Yang Yuhuan to death. The famous Battle of Suiyang is also featured in the novel in the later chapters and many heroes sacrifice themselves in the battle. Tie, Han Zhifen and others continue their heroic legacy by recruiting heroes to help in suppressing the rebellion.

Adaptations
In 2008, the novel was adapted into a Chinese television series titled *Paladins in Troubled Times* by producer Zhang Jizhong. It starred Victor Huang, Shen Xiaohai, He Zhuoyan, Liu Tianyue, TAE and Lu Chen.

Source (edited): "http://en.wikipedia.org/wiki/Datang_Youxia_Zhuan"

Liang Yusheng

This is a Chinese name; the family name is Chen.

Chen Wentong (simplified Chinese: 陈文统; traditional Chinese: 陳文統; pinyin: *Chén Wéntǒng*; 5 April 1926 – 22 January 2009), better known by his pen name **Liang Yusheng** (Chinese: 梁羽生; pinyin: *Liáng Yǔshēng*), is a Chinese writer of wuxia fiction.

He is credited as the pioneer of the "new school" (新派) wuxia genre in the 20th century, as well as one of the three most esteemed wuxia writers in the second half of the 20th century (the other two being Jin Yong and Gu Long).

Biography
Chen was born in Mengshan, Guangxi,

China in 1926. He came from a family of scholars and was well versed in ancient Chinese classics and Duilian. He could recite the Three Hundred Tang Poems at the age of seven. While studying in Guilin High School in Guangxi, he started writing poems. He went to Mengshan during the Japanese invasion. He was tutored by Jian Youwen, who was well versed in the history of the Taiping Rebellion, and Rao Zongyi, who was good in poetry, humanities, art and the history of Dunhuang. Chen learnt history and literature from both of them and entered Lingnan University in Guangzhou later. In 1949, he settled in Hong Kong and became an editor for the newspaper *Ta Kung Pao* and a member of the executive committee through the principal's recommendation. The next year, he was sent to work in the *Sin Wun Pao* newspaper as a copy editor.

In 1954, Chen's major breakthrough in his career when he wrote his first wuxia novel *Longhu Dou Jinghua* to entertain readers due to an ongoing contest between two schools of martial arts, which was the talk of the town that year. This marked the start of the new generation of wuxia novels, with Chen as its pioneer and the emergence of other wuxia writers such as Louis Cha (Jin Yong). Over his writing career, Chen wrote a total of 33 wuxia novels, of which *Baifa Monü Zhuan* (白髮魔女傳) and *Yunhai Yugong Yuan* (雲海玉弓緣) are some of the more well known ones. Many of his novels have been adapted into television series and films. As a multitalented writer interested in history and literature, he wrote columns, critiques and essays under different names including **Liang Hueru** and **Fong Yuning**.

In the 1980s, Chen retired to Sydney, Australia with his family. In August 2004, he was granted an Honorary Doctorate by Hong Kong's Lingnan University, from where he originally graduated in 1948 in economics..

In 2005, film producer Tsui Hark adapted Chen's *Qijian Xia Tianshan* (七劍下天山) into the film *Seven Swords* and its derived television series counterpart *Seven Swordsmen*. The 1993 film *The Bride with White Hair* is also an adaptation of Chen's *Baifa Monü Zhuan*.

After suffering a stroke during a visit to Hong Kong in 2007, Chen died in Sydney on January 22, 2009 of natural causes.

Style of writing

The opening of Chen's novels are always marked with a poem, which signified his interest in poetry. The protagonists of his novels are also multi-talented, versatile and interested in literature. Chen also infuses historical elements into his fictional stories, a style which was later followed by other wuxia writers such as Jin Yong. Unlike many wuxia writers, Chen does not regard Shaolin and Wudang as the leading sects in the *wulin*. Instead, he features the Mount Heaven Sect as the leading sect.

Source (edited): "http://en.wikipedia.org/wiki/Liang_Yusheng"

Qijian Xia Tianshan

Qijian Xia Tianshan is a *wuxia* novel by Liang Yusheng. It was written between 1956 and 1957 and contains 31 chapters. It is also linked to Liang Yusheng's *Saiwai Qixia Zhuan* and *Baifa Monü Zhuan*.

Plot

The prologue serves as a continuation of Yang Yuncong and Nalan Minghui's love story in *Saiwai Qixia Zhuan*. Nalan is forced to marry Prince Dodo, even though she loves Yang and has bore him a daughter. Yang shows up on the night before Nalan's wedding and seizes their infant daughter from her. He is mortally wounded in a fight against Dodo's henchmen and before his death, he entrusts his daughter to the youth Liang Mulang, who was attempting suicide after being mistakenly accused of betraying his comrades. Mulang brings Yang's daughter back to Yang's teacher, Reverend Huiming, on Mount Heaven.

Mulang spends eighteen years training under Huiming's tutelage and becomes a formidable pugilist. He returns to the *jianghu* under his new alias, "Ling Weifeng", as a highly revered hero. Yang Yuncong's daughter, Yilan Zhu, has mastered the "Mount Heaven Swordplay", and she swears to kill Dodo and avenge her father. On Mount Wutai, members of the anti-Qing Dynasty Heaven and Earth Society and some Southern Ming rebels attempt to assassinate Dodo but their plans are interrupted by Yilan Zhu's untimely appearance. During the chaos, Yilan Zhu unintentionally causes Zhang Huazhao to be captured by Qing soldiers. She goes to Dodo's residence to rescue Zhang later.

Meanwhile, Fu Qingzhu and Mao Wanlian discover that the long-lost Shunzhi Emperor is still alive and has become a monk on Mount Wutai. Shunzhi's son, the Kangxi Emperor, murders his father secretly to safeguard his throne. On Ling Weifeng's part, he meets his old crush, Liu Yufang, who wrongly accused him of betrayal years ago. Even though Ling's appearance has changed, Liu still notices that he bears some resemblance to Mulang, but he refuses to admit that he is indeed Mulang. Ling and Liu travel to Yunnan later and befriend Li Siyong, a descendant of Li Zicheng. They also encounter Fu Qingzhu and Mao Wanlian, as well as Gui Zhongming, a new companion. Gui falls in love with Mao after she helps him recover from his mental illness.

Gui and Mao go to Beijing later to find Yilan Zhu and they meet the scholar Nalan Rongruo. In the meantime, Nalan Minghui recognizes Yilan Zhu as her daughter and she pleads with Dodo to spare her daughter's life. After much difficulty, Yilan Zhu and Zhang Huazhao escape from danger and they fall in love. Yilan Zhu avenges her father later by assassinating Dodo, but is captured and imprisoned. Nalan Minghui is unable to rescue her daughter and commits suicide in despair. In the nick of time, "Flying Red Sash" Hamaya (a former love rival of Nalan) and Ling Weifeng appear and save Yilan Zhu.

Ling Weifeng suddenly experiences a seizure in a fight against Chu Zhaonan, his treacherous and evil senior. Chu turns the tables on Ling and captures and imprisons him in an underground labyrinth in Tibet. Ling attempts to escape but fails and is on the brink of death. He writes a letter to Liu Yufang, admitting that he is indeed Mulang. Liu is heartbroken upon reading Ling's letter. Han Zhibang, who has a secret crush on Liu, bravely sacrifices himself to save Ling and dies at the hands of Chu. Fu Qingzhu and the other heroes break into the labyrinth to rescue Ling. Chu is defeated by Yilan Zhu and commits suicide eventually.

Ling Weifeng, Zhang Huazhao, Gui Zhongming, Yilan Zhu, Mao Wanlian, Wu Qiongyao, and Hamaya form the "Seven Swords" of Mount Heaven, with Liu Yufang as a close ally. They leave behind a heroic legacy of upholding righteousness and helping the poor.

Characters

- Ling Weifeng (凌未風) - nicknamed "Holy Light of Mount Heaven" (天山神芒) after his famous *anqi* (projectile weapon). Years ago, he was tricked into revealing the identities of the anti-Qing rebels. He attempted suicide in guilt after being slapped and accused by Liu Yufang, but refrained from doing so upon encountering the dying Yang Yuncong. He follows Yang's instructions and brings Yang's orphaned daughter to Reverend Huiming. He becomes Huiming's third disciple and emerges as a formidable swordsman years later. However, he has a strong tendency to suffer from seizures when exposed to the cold. This becomes his fatal weakness, as he experiences a sudden seizure during a fight with Chu Zhaonan, when he is just about to kill Chu. Chu turns the tables on him and captures him, imprisoning him in a labyrinth in Tibet. Chu also cuts off his right thumb, preventing him from using a sword again. He survives his ordeal and continues his heroic quest as a Mount Heaven swordsman dedicated to upholding justice and helping the poor.
- Gui Zhongming (桂仲明) - son of Shi Tiancheng. He is adopted by Gui Tianlan and takes on his stepfather's surname. He is drawn into the conflict between his father and stepfather, and goes berserk after thinking that he had killed his father in his rage. He loses memory of his past and starts sleepwalking, during which he attacks people without knowing. He meets Mao Wanlian and Fu Qingzhu, who help to cure him of his mental illness and reunite him with his family. He falls in love with Mao and becomes extremely protective of her. Despite his formidable prowess in swordplay and *anqi*, he is reckless, nonchalant, easily agitated, and bereft of social etiquette. He becomes the founder of the northern branch of the Wudang Sect.
- Mao Wanlian (冒浣蓮) - Mao Pijiang and Dong Xiaowan's daughter. She was raised and tutored in martial arts by Fu Qingzhu. She meets Gui Zhongming, who was suffering from hallucinations then, and helps him recover from his mental illness and reunite him with his family. Gui falls in love with her and becomes extremely protective of her. Just like her parents, she is talented in poetry and literary arts. She develops a close relationship with Nalan Rongruo because of their common interest. She marries Gui Zhongming eventually.
- Yilan Zhu (易蘭珠) - Yang Yuncong and Nalan Minghui's daughter. She was brought to Mount Heaven by Ling Weifeng, and raised and tutored in martial arts by him and Reverend Huiming. She assassinates Prince Dodo to avenge her father, but is captured and imprisoned. She becomes Zhang Huazhao's love interest and marries him eventually.
- Zhang Huazhao (張華昭) - son of Zhang Huangyan. He attempts to assassinate Dodo on Mount Wutai but fails due to Yilan Zhu's untimely interruption. He falls in love with Yilan Zhu and goes through troubles to save her from death. In addition to his reunion with Yilan Zhu after she is rescued by Hamaya, he also learns a set of *qinggong* techniques from the White Haired Demoness. He marries Yilan Zhu at the end of the novel, and also joins the Wudang Sect as Gui Zhongming's junior, becoming a master in the "Bodhidharma Swordplay".
- Wu Qiongyao (武瓊瑤) - Wu Yuanying's daughter. By chance, she encounters the White Haired Demoness, who likes her and accepts her as a disciple. Despite studying martial arts only for three years under the Demoness' tutelage, she emerges as a powerful swordswoman. She marries Li Siyong eventually and bears him a son and a daughter. She settles on Mount Heaven with her children after her husband's death.
- Hamaya (哈瑪雅) - nicknamed "Flying Red Sash" (飛紅巾). She is a disciple of the White Haired Demoness and a former love rival of Nalan Minghui in *Saiwai Qixia Zhuan*. Her hair turned white overnight after Yang Yuncong rejected her. She resolves her rivalry with Nalan and saves Yilan Zhu from death. She transfers her love for Yang Yuncong to Yilan Zhu and treats the latter like her daughter. She returns to her former position as leader of the tribal people of Xinjiang at the end of the novel.
- Liu Yufang (劉郁芳) - Liu Jingyi's daughter, nicknamed "Brocade Cloud Sword" (雲錦劍). She leads the rebels to resist Dodo's forces in Hangzhou. She succeeds Han Zhibang as leader of the Heaven and Earth Society later. She becomes a "Friend of Mount Heaven" (an ally of the Seven Swords) at the end of the novel.

Adaptations

Films

In 1959, Hong Kong's Emei Film Company produced a film titled *Seven Swordsmen Leave Tianshan* based on the novel. It starred Cheung Wood-yau, Law Yim-hing, Lam Kau, Hoh Bik-gin, Shek Sau, Yeung Fan and Yeung Yip-wang.

The 2005 wuxia epic film *Seven Swords*, directed by Tsui Hark, features seven sword fighters, each wielding a special sword, departing from Mount Heaven to save a village under attack by a ruthless warlord. The seven swords are: *The Dragon* (由龍), *The Transience* (青干), *The Star Chasers* (競星), *The Celestial Beam* (日月), *The Deity* (舍神), *The Heaven's Fall* (天瀑) and *The Unlearnt* (莫問). Except for some characters' names, the story and the seven swords are not related to the novel. Donnie Yen, Leon Lai, Charlie Yeung, Lu Yi and Sun Honglei starred in the leading roles.

Television

In 2006, Tsui Hark produced *Seven Swordsmen*, a television series counterpart to *Seven Swords*. It starred Vincent Zhao, Wang Xuebing, Ray Lui, Ada Choi, Qiao Zhenyu, Li Xiaoran, Wang Likun and Bryan Leung. The story is based more on *Saiwai Qixia Zhuan*, the novel preceding *Qijian Xia Tianshan*, even though it shares the same Chinese title as the latter.

Comics

In 2006, Chinese manhua artists Guangzu (光祖) and Niu Tongxue (牛同學) released a comic of the same Chinese title as the novel.

Source (edited): "http://en.wikipedia.org/wiki/Qijian_Xia_Tianshan"

Saiwai Qixia Zhuan

Saiwai Qixia Zhuan is a *wuxia* novel by Liang Yusheng. It was first published in China in January 1984. The novel is closely related to another of Liang's works, *Qijian Xia Tianshan* and *Baifa Monü Zhuan*.

Plot

The story is set in the early Qing Dynasty during the reign of the Shunzhi Emperor. The ethnic minority tribes in present-day Xinjiang are under attack by the Qing army, which is attempting to force them into submission. Yang Yuncong helps the tribal people resist the invaders and becomes a revered hero in the region. However, Yang is betrayed and attacked by his junior, Chu Zhaonan, who has defected to the Qing side. During the ensuing fight, they encounter a sandstorm. Yang is injured and loses consciousness, but is saved by Nalan Minghui, the daughter of a Qing general named Nalan Xiuji. She nurses him back to health and helps him escape from danger.

After leaving Nalan Minghui, Yang Yuncong meets "Flying Red Sash" Hamaya, a legendary heroine in the Xinjiang region. Hamaya's lover, the singer Yabulu, had betrayed their tribe and caused the death of her father. Hamaya seeks vengeance on Yabulu, captures him and brings him back to her tribe for punishment. Along the way, they are ambushed by Chu Zhaonan and Qing soldiers. Yang and Hamaya defeat and capture Chu, but Yang releases Chu on account of their past senior-junior relationship. Back in Hamaya's tribe, her fellow tribesmen find Yabulu guilty and want him dead. Hamaya suppresses her sorrow, and personally kills Yabulu to deliver justice. With Yang's help, Hamaya emerges as champion in a martial arts contest and is elected to be the new chief of her tribe. By then, Hamaya has secretly developed romantic feelings for Yang.

Yang continues to help Hamaya and her people fight the Qing army. During this time, he meets Nalan Minghui again and they fall in love with each other. However, Yang and Nalan are not fated to be together, because they stand on opposing sides. Besides, Nalan's parents have agreed to marry her to Prince Dodo, a Manchu noble. In grief, Nalan decides to consummate her romance with Yang, and eventually becomes pregnant with Yang's child.

On the other hand, Hamaya is also in love with Yang, and she has revealed her feelings to him, but he rejects her. Hamaya is heartbroken and her hair turns white overnight, just like her teacher, the "White Haired Demoness" Lian Nichang. Without Hamaya to lead them, the tribal people suffer a crushing defeat by Qing forces. In the meantime, Yang leaves Xinjiang after learning that Nalan Minghui and Prince Dodo's wedding is going to take place in Hangzhou soon. His eventual fate is revealed in *Qijian Xia Tianshan*.

Characters

- Yang Yuncong (楊雲驄)
- Hamaya (哈瑪雅) - nicknamed "Flying Red Sash" (飛紅巾)
- Nalan Minghui (納蘭明慧)

Adaptations

- In 1996, the novel is adapted into a Singaporean television series titled *Legend of the White Hair Brides*. It starred Huang Biren, Lina Ng and Ann Kok.
- In 2005, the novel and *Qijian Xia Tianshan* are adapted into a television series titled *Seven Swordsmen*. It was produced by Tsui Hark, directed by Clarence Fok, and starred Vincent Zhao, Wang Xuebing, Ray Lui, Ada Choi, Qiao Zhenyu, Li Xiaoran and Wang Likun.

Source (edited): "http://en.wikipedia.org/wiki/Saiwai_Qixia_Zhuan"

Xiagu Danxin

Xiagu Danxin is a *wuxia* novel by Liang Yusheng. It was serialized by Liang Yusheng in the Hong Kong *Sin Wan Pao* newspaper between 5 October 1967 and 20 June 1969. The story is a sequel to *Yunhai Yugong Yuan*, another *wuxia* novel by Liang Yusheng.

Plot

The story follows the adventures of Jin Zhuliu, son of Jin Shiyi and Gu Zhihua, the protagonists of *Yunhai Yugong Yuan*. At the age of 20, Jin leaves the island he was raised on, and travels to the Chinese mainland alone in search of adventure. He roams the *jianghu* as a wandering swordsman, by upholding justice and helping the poor. At that time, China is in the late Ming Dynasty and the Han Chinese face the threat of invaders from Manchuria in the north. Jin performs a series of heroic acts that propel him to fame overnight.

Jin meets Shi Hongying, the younger sister of Shi Baidu, the evil leader of the Six Harmonies Sect, and falls in love with her. At the same time, he also meets Li Nanxing, the nephew of Li Shengnan, and becomes sworn brothers with him. Meanwhile, Shi Baidu pledges allegiance to the Manchu aristocrat Safuding and aims to help Safuding in conquering Ming China. Jin Zhuliu, Li Nanxing and other righteous pugilists combine forces to disrupt Safuding's birthday party and rob him of several precious gifts. Shi Baidu intends to marry his sister to the Manchu general Meng Xiong, but actually he wants to use her to lure Li Nanxing into a trap and kill Li. Li is wounded in a battle and is saved by Gongsun Hong of the Red Tassel Society. Li strikes up a romantic relationship with Gongsun's daughter, Gongsun Yan, later.

Shi Baidu is dissatisfied and tries to coerce his sister to marry Meng Xiong but Jin, Li and other pugilists disrupt the wedding and seize control of Meng's city. Shi is defeated and dies in humiliation. Shi Hongying succeeds her brother as leader of the Six Harmonies Society and they join a volunteer army, formed by pugilists who have sworn to defend Ming China from the Manchus. At one point, Li Nanxing falls off a cliff and is presumed to be dead. During his absence, some *jianghu* lowlifes reestablish the evil Heaven Demons' Cult once more and commit evil in his name. Jin is surprised to hear that his sworn brother is still alive and has become a villain. He investigates the case and meets Li, who has survived, by coincidence, and they defeat the villains together, clearing Li's name. Jin, Li and the righteous pugilists combine forces to foil the Manchus' plot to trick some tribal peoples from Qinghai to attack China. The story ends on a happy note for the protagonists, who receive their blessings from the *wulin*, as Jin Zhuliu is happily married to Shi Hongying while Li Nanxing is married to Gongsun Yan.

Characters

- Jin Zhuliu (金逐流)
- Li Nanxing (厲南星)
- Shi Hongying (史紅英)
- Gongsun Yan (公孫燕)
- Shi Baidu (史白都)
- Safuding (薩福鼎)
- Jin Shiyi (金拾遺)
- Gu Zhihua (谷之華)
- Li Shengnan (厲勝男)
- Li Fusheng (厲復生)
- Meng Xiong (孟雄)
- Gongsun Hong (公孫宏)
- Yuchi Tong (尉遲烱)
- Jiang Haitian (江海天)
- Wen Daozhuang (文道莊)
- Qin Yuanhao (秦元浩)
- Yang Hao (陽浩)

Adaptations

In 2006, the novel is adapted into a Chinese television series titled *The Patriotic Knights*, starring Chen Long as Jin Zhuliu, Stephanie Hsiao as Shi Hongying, Wallace Chung as Li Nanxing and He Meitian as Gongsun Yan (renamed to Zhong Yanyan in the series).
Source (edited): "http://en.wikipedia.org/wiki/Xiagu_Danxin"

List of Baifa Monü Zhuan characters

The following is a list of characters from Liang Yusheng's *wuxia* novel *Baifa Monü Zhuan*. Some of these characters also appear in *Saiwai Qixia Zhuan* and *Qijian Xia Tianshan*.

Main characters

- Lian Nichang (練霓裳) - nicknamed "Jade Rakshasa" (玉羅刹). She was raised by wolves as an infant and later adopted and tutored by Ling Muhua. Her prowess in swordplay and *qinggong* is legendary, and she uses her skills to deliver justice like a vigilante. Though beautiful in appearance, she is deadly, as her sword movements are extremely brutal and aggressive. She also metes out draconian punishments and torturous deaths to her enemies, causing her to be seen as a menacing demoness in the *jianghu*. She becomes known as the "White Haired Demoness" (白髮魔女) after her hair turns white.
- Zhuo Yihang (卓一航) - son of Zhuo Jixian. He comes from a family of scholars and grows up to become a cultured and refined gentleman. He learns swordplay from Taoist Ziyang and later succeeds the latter as leader of the Wudang Sect.
- Yue Mingke (岳鳴珂) – a military attaché serving under Xiong Tingbi. He was tutored in martial arts by Huo Tiandu and becomes a formidable swordsman. He joins the protagonists in opposing Wei Zhongxian, and becomes a fugitive after Xiong was wrongly put to death. He becomes disillusioned with human society after witnessing

the tragic death of Tie Shanhu and becomes a monk, renaming himself "Reverend Huiming" (晦明禪師). He travels to Mount Heaven and settles there, spending his time studying martial arts.

Wudang Sect (武當派)

- Five Elders of Wudang (武當五老)
  - Taoist Ziyang (紫陽道長) - leader of Wudang and Zhuo Yihang's teacher. He is highly respected by his contemporaries not only for his prowess in martial arts, but also for his humility. He is succeeded by Zhuo as leader of Wudang.
  - Taoist Huangye (黃葉道人)
  - Taoist Baishi (白石道人) - an egoistic and arrogant individual. He sees Lian Nichang as inferior and unworthy of Zhuo Yihang's love. He intends to marry his older daughter to Zhuo and often seeks to create opportunities for them to start a romance, but his daughter marries Li Shenshi eventually, much to his dismay. He is captured by the lamas of the Heaven Dragon Sect and brought to Fengsha Castle. Lian Nichang saves him but he is reluctant to thank her and simply agrees not to interfere in her relationship with Zhuo Yihang anymore.
  - Taoist Hongyun (紅雲道人)
  - Taoist Qingsuo (青蓑道人)
- He Qixia (何綺霞) - Baishi's younger sister. She becomes a nun on Mount Song and adopts the name "Abbess Cihui" (慈慧師太) after her husband divorces her to purse his career. She hates Li and refuses to leave with him when he attempts to sweet-talk her into returning to him. She eventually reconciles with her husband with help from her son.
- Baishi's daughters - they are raised by their aunt and tutored in martial arts
  - He E'hua (何萼華) - the older one. She is in love with her cousin Li Shenshi, who was her childhood playmate. Her father wants her to marry Zhuo Yihang, who comes from a more prestigious family background, but he eventually agrees to her marriage with Li Shenshi.
  - He Lühua (何綠華) - she joins Zhuo Yihang on his quest to rescue her father from Fengsha Castle
- Geng Shaonan (耿紹南) - specializes in using the slingshot. As he comes from a prestigious sect, he behaves rudely and arrogantly. He is defeated by Lian Nichang in a duel and has two fingers sliced off by her as punishment for his snobbishness. He instigates Zhuo Yihang to attack Lian when Lian was dueling with the four elders. Zhuo, in a confused state, takes the slingshot from Geng, and fires at Lian, causing Lian to misbelieve that Zhuo has betrayed her love and turned against her.
- Yu Xincheng (虞新城) - the oldest of the second generation students
- Li Feng (李封) - the most senior of Wudang's members in Beijing

Tie Feilong and associates

- Tie Feilong (鐵飛龍) - master of the Tie Family Manor. He is not placed in high regard by the orthodox sects because of his ugly appearance and eccentric personality. Despite this, he is an experienced and formidable pugilist, specializing in palm styles of martial arts. He accepts Lian Nichang as his goddaughter after resolving a misunderstanding with her, and accompanies her on most of her adventures.
- Mu Jiuniang (穆九娘) - Tie Feilong's second wife and Tie Shanhu's stepmother. She obtains Ling Muhua's swordplay manual from the dying Zhenqian by chance and keeps it for herself. She shows it to Tie Shanhu and they practise the skills inside secretly behind Tie Feilong's back. She is expelled from the family after her husband finds out that she had stolen the manual. She meets Gongsun Lei later, marries him and bears him a child. She is severely wounded by Gongsun's enemies and dies from her injuries after entrusting her child to Tie Feilong, telling him to adopt her child as his grandson.
- Tie Shanhu (鐵珊瑚) - Tie Feilong's daughter. She falls in love with Yue Mingke but Yue unknowingly hurts her when he expresses reluctance to marry her. She is taken hostage by Jin Duyi and Ying Xiuyang, who attempt to force Yue Mingke to surrender to them. She breaks free from Jin's clutches by attacking him, but is also mortally wounded in the process. She dies in peace after Yue finally admits his love for her.
- Ke Pingting (客娉婷) - the illegitimate daughter of Wei Zhongxian and Madam Ke, and a disciple of Gongsun Daniang. She admires Lian Nichang and desires to become a wandering heroine too. She overhears a secret conversation between her parents and learn that Wei Zhongxian is actually her father. She becomes disappointed when she discovers that her father is actually a traitor and decides to leave her parents for good. She joins the protagonists and becomes Tie Feilong's second goddaughter later.

Wang family and associates

- Wang Jiayin (王嘉胤) - leader of the bandit community in northern Shanxi. He is killed in action during a battle against the imperials.
- Wang Zhaoxi (王照希) - son of Wang Jiayin and a close friend of Zhuo Yihang
- Meng Can (孟燦) - Wang Jiayin's sworn brother. He serves as a martial arts instructor in the crown prince's residence. He is implicated in the Case of the Palace Assault and arrested and tortured during interrogation. He is released after his name is cleared, but dies from his wounds.
- Meng Qiuxia (孟秋霞) - Meng Can's daughter. She marries Wang Zhaoxi.
- Bai Min (白敏) - one of Meng Can's students. He joins Li Zicheng's rebel army later.
- Liu Ximing (柳西銘) - a martial arts instructor and ally of the

protagonists
- Wang Jiayin's followers
  - Wang Zuogua (王左掛)
  - Flying Mountain Tiger (飛山虎)
  - Great Red Wolf (大紅狼)

Royals and nobles

- Wanli Emperor (萬厲皇帝) - ruler of the Ming Dynasty
- Zhu Changluo (朱常洛) - crown prince during Wanli's reign. He uncovers the truth behind the Case of the Palace Assault and helps to clear the names of innocent people who were implicated in the case. He ascends to the throne as the Taichang Emperor later. He suffers from poor health and eventually dies from poisoning after consuming the mysterious Red Pills.
- Zhu Changxun (朱常洵) - younger son of Wanli. He plans with his mother and uncle to seize the succession to the throne from his older half-brother through the Case of the Palace Assault. The plot fails when Wei Zhongxian betrays him. He is demoted to the status of a commoner and imprisoned for life.
- Consort Zheng (鄭貴妃) - Zhu Changxun's mother. She is imprisoned after the plot fails.
- Royal Uncle Zheng (鄭國舅) - Consort Zheng's older brother. He is executed after the plot fails
- Consort Li (李選侍) - Taichang's favorite concubine
- Tianqi Emperor (天啟皇帝) - the young, naive and inexperienced successor to Taichang. He has a crush on Madame Ke and she uses his weakness to manipulate him and usurp state power together with Wei Zhongxian. Like his father, he suffers from poor health and eventually dies from illness.
- Chongzhen Emperor (崇禎皇帝) - younger son of Taichang and successor to Tianqi. He is wiser and more ambitious than his predecessors. When he was still a noble, he was already rallying a group of loyalists to support him and help him save the country from collapse. He eliminates Wei Zhongxian and his clique after ascending to the throne.

Wei Zhongxian and associates

- Wei Zhongxian (魏忠賢) - the chief eunuch and primary nemesis of the protagonists. He usurps state power after the death of the Taichang Emperor and persecutes loyalists. He is put to death when Chongzhen ascends to the throne.
- Madam Ke (客氏) - has a secret affair with Wei Zhongxian and bore him a daughter. Wei became a palace eunuch later while she became the young Tianqi Emperor's wet nurse. She is expelled from the palace after Chongzhen comes to the throne.

Jin Duyi and associates

- Jin Duyi (金獨異) - the morally bankrupt husband of Gongsun Daniang. He collaborates with Wei Zhongxian's men to harm the protagonists and attempts to trick his wife into joining him. He specializes in using the "Yin Wind Venomous Gravel Palm" (陰風毒砂掌), which allows him to poison a victim with a slow-acting venom, without the victim knowing, and kill him within seven days. He is slain by Yue Mingke after killing Tie Shanhu.
- Gongsun Daniang (公孫大娘) - nicknamed "Red Flower Devil Mother" (紅花鬼母). She is seduced by Jin Duyi and steals her father's martial arts manual after being instigated by Jin. She marries Jin later and helps him defeat a group of 13 pugilists once. She decides to leave him after he refuses to mend his ways, and leads a reclusive life for three decades. Tie Feilong and Lian Nichang barely managed to defeat her after careful planning. She commits suicide in shame when Yue Mingke reveals her husband's evil deeds after avenging Tie Shanhu.
- Gongsun Lei (公孫雷) - son of Jin Duyi and Gongsun Daniang. He marries Mu Jiuniang. He follows in his evil father's footsteps after his mother dies. He rapes an escort soldier's wife, causing her to hang herself in shame. He is forced to commit suicide by Huo Yuanzhong and company.
- Gongsun Yiyang (公孫一陽) - father of Gongsun Daniang. He is a reclusive master of martial arts and toxicology. He dies in anger after discovering that his daughter and Jin Duyi had betrayed him and stolen his martial arts manual.
- Jin Qianyan (金千岩) - an imperial guard and Jin Duyi's nephew. He learns the "Yin Wind Venomous Gravel Palm" from his uncle, but is less skillful in using it. He murders Taoist Zhenqian and steals the swordplay manual left behind by Ling Muhua. He is killed by Shen Dayuan.
- Hao Jianchang (郝建昌) - Jin Duyi's oldest disciple. He makes a surprise attack on Taoist Baishi and injures him severely.

Jianghu figures

- Yun Yanping (雲燕平) - an imperial guard. He specializes in using a Tibetan style of "soft" attack.
- Changqin (昌欽) - a Tibetan lama hired by Wei Zhongxian to be Tianqi's bodyguard. He uses a pair of cymbals as his weapons. He joins Mengsasi's tribe after Wei's downfall.
- Rong Yidong (容一東) - Ying Xiuyang's accomplice. He appears to help Ying and the Wang brothers rob Tangnu, but Lian Nichang shows up to save Tangnu. He is slain by Lian.
- Hu Mai (胡邁) - nicknamed "Ground Deity" (陸上仙). He and Meng Fei rely on boasting and lying to trick others into showing sympathy towards them. They produce the Red Pills and present them to Taichang through Li Kezhuo. The emperor dies from poisoning after consuming the pills.
- Meng Fei (孟飛) - nicknamed "Divine Hand" (神手)

Manchu spies

- Zheng Hongtai (鄭洪台) - a secret service agent. Zhu Changluo sends

him to escort Zhuo Yihang home. Zhuo discovers later that he is actually a spy working for the Manchus. He is defeated by Lian Nichang and captured by Yue Mingke. Lian forces him to reveal the names of his accomplices through torture and kills him afterwards.
- Ying Xiuyang (應修陽) - murdered Luo Jinfeng. He escapes after he is defeated by Lian Nichang on Mount Hua. He becomes part of Wei Zhongxian's political clique later and causes trouble for the protagonists on numerous instances. He is tricked into consuming drugged wine by Ke Pingting, and bound and sent to Lian Nichang. He is killed by Tie Feilong after Lian forces him to list the names of his accomplices.
- Lian Chenghu (連城虎) - chief manager of Western Factory (西廠). He joins Mengsasi's tribe after Wei Zhongxian's downfall. He is slain by Lian Nichang.

Officials

- Fang Congzhe (方從哲) - the chancellor
- Li Kezhuo (李可灼) - the *honglu sicheng* (鴻臚寺丞). He presents the Red Pills to the Taichang Emperor and causes the emperor to die from poisoning. Wei Zhongxian and Fang Congzhe help him cover up the case and he gets rewarded for his attempt to "cure" the emperor instead.
- Cui Chengxiu (崔呈秀) - one of Wei Zhongxian's followers. Wei sends him to read a false imperial edict about Xiong's alleged treason and failure in duties, and arrest Xiong later. He is driven away by Xiong and the protagonists.
- Pan Ruzhen (潘汝貞) - Inspector of Zhejiang. He suggests building a memorial structure to Wei Zhongxian.
- Wang Shaohui (王紹徽) - writes the *Records of Generals* (點將錄), which lists the names of Wei Zhongxian's political opponents
- Xu Xianchun (許顯純) - Wei Zhongxian's godson. He oversees the secret murder of Yang Lian in prison.
- Wei Guangzheng (魏廣徵) - Wei Zhongxian's nephew
- Ruan Dazhen (阮大鋮)
- Gu Qian (顧謙)
- Fu Yue (傅櫆)
- Ni Wenhuan (倪文煥)
- Yang Weiyuan (楊維垣)
- Lu Wanling (陸萬零)

Pugilists hired by Zheng Hongtai

- Zhao Ting (趙挺) - from the Songyang Sect. He leaves after realizing that he is tricked into helping the spies.
- Fan Zhu (范築) - killed by Lian Nichang
- Ling Xiao (凌霄) - nicknamed "Jade Faced Demonic Fox" (玉面妖狐). He is killed by Lian Nichang.
- Taoist Qingsong (青松道人) - leaves after realizing that he is tricked into helping the Manchu spies

Government officials

- Xiong Tingbi (熊廷弼) - a military governor (經略) in Liaodong. He is in charge of defending the northern border from the Manchu invaders and is seen as a hero in the eyes of the common people. He suffers a defeat by the Manchus when Wang Huazhen refuses to cooperate with him, and is executed for his defeat. Before his death, he wrote a book titled *Discussion on Liaodong* (遼東論), explaining his "Three Deployments Strategy" (三方布置策) to counter the Manchu invasion.
- Three Departments and Six Ministries
  - Sun Shenxing (孫慎行) - Minister of Rites
  - Zhou Jiamo (周嘉謨) - Minister of Personnel
  - Hui Shiyang (惠世揚) - *geishizhong* (給事中)
  - Ministry of War
    - Yang Kun (楊焜) - Minister of War
    - Li Jingbai (李精白) - Minister of War
    - Liu Guojin (劉國縉) - *zhushi* (主事)
    - Liu Tingyuan (劉廷元) - *geishizhong*
    - Yang Lian (楊漣) - *geishizhong*. A loyalist, he opposes Wei Zhongxian but is framed and imprisoned later. Lian Nichang breaks into prison to save him but he refuses her help. He is secretly murdered in prison by Wei's lackeys later.
    - Sun Chengzong (孫承宗)
- Censorate
  - Yao Zongwen (姚宗文)
  - Feng Sanyuan (馮三元)
  - Wang Anshun (王安舜)
  - Zou Yuanbiao (鄒元標)
  - Zuo Guangdou (左光斗) - Du Mingzhong's uncle. He is murdered in prison by Wei Zhongxian's men, along with Yang Lian and a few other loyalists.
- Military
  - Wang Zan (王贊) - Xiong Tingbi's bodyguard. He is a disciple of Qiu Taixu.
  - Wang Huazhen (王化貞) - appointed by Xiong Tingbi as Inspector of Guangning. He is unwilling to cooperate with Xiong, causing the Ming army to be defeated by the Manchus. He is demoted after his defeat.
  - Yuan Yingtai (袁應泰) - sent to replace Xiong Tingbi after the latter's death. He is incompetent and suffers defeats at the hands of the Manchus.
  - He Shixian (賀世賢) - Yuan Yingtai's subordinate. He is killed in action along with You Shigong.
  - You Shigong (尤世功)
  - Yuan Chonghuan (袁崇煥) - a general who succeeds Xiong Tingbi as defender of Ming China's northern border. He receives Xiong's book *Discussion on Liaodong* from Lian Nichang.
- Imperial envoys - both of them are infected with a slow-acting poison by Jin Qianyan. Jin hopes that they

will die from poisoning days later in Zhuo Yihang's house, so that he can frame Zhuo for murdering the envoys. However, Zhuo notices that the envoys are poisoned and he saves them.
- Imperial Envoy Li (李欽差)
- Imperial Envoy Zhou (周欽差)
- Eunuchs
  - Pang Bao (龐保) - a high-ranking eunuch. He and Liu Cheng are implicated in the Case of the Palace Assault and executed. They are replaced by Wei Zhongxian.
  - Liu Cheng (劉成)
- Long Chengye (龍成業) - Inner Court Colonel (內廷校尉)
- Tian Ergeng (田爾耕) - Governor of Nine Gates (九門提督)
- Ye Xianggao (葉向高) - succeeds Fang Congzhe as chancellor
- Wang Bingbei (王兵備) - leads a group of soldiers to arrest Zhuo Yihang when the latter is accused of murdering the two imperial envoys
- Hong Chengchou (洪承疇)
- Chen Qiyu (陳奇瑜)
- Wei Dazhong (魏大中)
- Gu Dazhang (顧大章)
- Yuan Huazhong (袁化中)
- Zhou Chaorui (周朝瑞)

Jinyi Wei (錦衣衛)

- Li Tianyang (李天揚) - He Qixia's ex-husband. He divorces his wife in order to pursue his official career by marrying a general's daughter. He becomes a Jinyi Wei commander later. He returns and attempts to sweet-talk his ex-wife into returning home with him but she refuses. He is happy to be reunited with his son and decides to give up his post. He releases his son and the other captives from prison. He manages to reconcile with his wife with help from his son.
- Shi Hao (石浩) - a Jinyi Wei commander. He is killed by Zhuo Yihang.
- Hu Guozhu (胡國柱) - Li Tianyang's escort. He is defeated by He E'hua in a fight.
- Commander Qin (秦指揮) - escorts imperial envoys Li and Zhou to Zhuo Yihang's house
- Cui Yingyuan (崔應元) - a Jinyi Wei commander present at the scene of Yang Lian's murder. He secretly memorizes Yang's final statement and spreads it among the common people, causing Yang to be remembered in history as a loyal subject.

Palace guards

- Cheng Kun (成坤) - a guard commander loyal to Taichang. He is arrested and imprisoned by Wei Zhongxian after suspecting that the emperor was poisoned to death. Wei agrees to release him after his colleagues promise to persuade him to make a false statement about the emperor's death. He refuses and is immobilized by them. Yue Mingke saves him when he is about to be killed. To express his gratitude, he presents Yue with a pair of precious combat gloves that can protect the wearer from sharp weapons and poison. He joins the protagonists' side in the fight against Wei Zhongxian's clique later.
- Wang Cheng (王成) - Cheng Kun's deputy. He betrays Cheng and defects to Wei Zhongxian. He is knocked unconscious by Yue Mingke when he is about to kill Cheng.
- Dong Fang (董方) - an old colleague of Cheng Kun. Although he is not on good terms with Cheng, he is unwilling to harm the latter. He suggests creating a fake scene that Cheng had committed suicide by hanging himself, intending to release Cheng secretly later. However, before he could do so, he is immobilized by Wei's lackey, who has been hiding nearby and listening to his conversation with Wang Cheng.
- Wang Tingfu (王廷福) - tasked with escorting Tangnu. He collaborates with Ying Xiuyang to rob Tangnu. He is killed by Lian Nichang when she appears to help Tangnu.
- Wang Tinglu (王廷祿) - Wang Tingfu's twin brother. He is killed by Tangnu's bodyguard.
- Huang Biao (黃彪) - chief manager of Madam Ke's living quarters
- Bai Guangsi (白廣思) - a martial arts instructor in Zhu Youjian's residence

Rebels

Li Zicheng and associates

- Li Zicheng (李自成) - nicknamed "Young Dashing King" (小闖王). He meets Lian Nichang after the latter saves Tangnu from Ying Xiuyang and the robbers. Lian is impressed by his charisma and has a feeling that he will become an emperor in future.
- Gao Yingxiang (高迎祥) - nicknamed "Dashing King" (闖王). He is Li Zicheng's uncle.
- Li Yan (李岩) - Li Jingbai's son. He was tutored in martial arts by Wang Tong of the Taiji Sect. He decides to join the rebels after his father dies at the hands of Wei Zhongxian's clique.
- Red Lady (紅娘子) - Li Yan's wife. Like Lian Nichang, she used to lead an all-female bandit clan before her marriage to Li Yan.
- Li Guo (李過) - Li Zicheng's nephew
- Gao Jie (高傑) - Gao Yingxiang's subordinate
- Du Wu (杜五) - nicknamed "Night Cat" (夜貓子). He is killed along with Zhang Si by the Shen brothers after refusing to submit to Zhang Xianzhong.
- Zhang Si (張四) - nicknamed "Sky Shooting Condor" (射天雕)

Zhang Xianzhong and associates

- Zhang Xianzhong (張獻忠) - a rebel leader from Sichuan nicknamed "Eight Great King" (八大王). Cruel and greedy, he plundered cities and conducted many massacres.
- Shen brothers - two brothers who have zombie-like appearances, but are highly skilled in martial arts. They serve Zhang Xianzhong but are

not very loyal to their master. They defect to join Cheng Zhangwu later and appear at Fengsha Castle towards the end of the novel. They are slain by Lian Nichang.
- Shen Dayuan (神大元)
- Shen Yiyuan (神一元)

Manchus

- Nurhachi (努爾哈赤) - leader of the Manchus. He leads his army to attack Ming China's northern border.
- Chaketu (察克圖) - a warrior sent by Nurhachi to persuade Yuan Chonghuan to defect to the Manchus. He is slain by Lian Nichang.
- Ketu (科圖) - an envoy sent by Nurhachi to meet the tribal peoples of Xinjiang

Tribal peoples

- Mengsasi (孟薩思) - chief of the Keda'er (喀達爾) tribe
- Kazakh (哈薩克) tribe
  - Balong (巴龍) - deputy chief of the tribe. He joins forces with Zhuo Yihang to deal with Tiande Shangren.
  - Hachuan (哈川)
  - Longhu Yatu (龍呼雅圖)
  - Xin Wu (辛五) - a hunter living on Mount Heaven
  - Xin Longzi (辛龍子) - Xin Wu's young son. He is grateful to Zhuo Yihang for saving him from Tiande Shangren and becomes Zhuo's disciple. He and his father agree to help Zhuo guard the magical flower that can turn white hair black again.
- Luobu (羅布) tribe
  - Tangma (唐瑪) - chief of the tribe
  - Tangnu (唐努) - Tangma's son. In an earlier chapter, his father sends him as an envoy to pay tribute to the Ming emperor. Ying Xiuyang plots with the Wang brothers to rob him, but their plan is foiled by Lian Nichang and Tie Shanhu. Tangnu succeeds his father as chief of his tribe later. He is grateful to Lian Nichang for saving him earlier and lets his daughter learn martial arts from Lian.
  - Hamaya (哈瑪雅) - Tangnu's young daughter. She is nicknamed "Flying Red Sash" (飛紅巾). She is held hostage by Tiande Shangren during the tribal chiefs' meeting. She uses a martial arts move, taught to her by Lian Nichang, to attack Tiande and break free from his clutches. The strike would have been fatal to Tiande if she was older.

Shaolin Sect (少林派)

- Jingming (鏡明) - abbot of Shaolin. He tests Yue Mingke's neigong.
- Zunsheng (尊聖) - an elder of Shaolin. He spars with Yue Mingke in a fist-fighting contest and they arrive at a draw.
- Xuantong (玄通) - a student of Zunsheng. He specializes in using *anqi* (projectile weapons). He loses to Yue Mingke in a contest.
- Tianyuan (天元) - the most senior student of Jingming. He uses a monk's spade in combat. He loses to Yue Mingke in a contest. He succeeds Jingming as abbot of Shaolin later.
- Novice monk (小沙彌) - unknown name. He spars with Yue Mingke in a contest of palm style martial arts but loses even when Yue shows leniency.

Emei Sect (峨嵋派)

- Long Xiaoyun (龍嘯雲) - ex-lover of He Qixia. He teaches Li Shenshi martial arts.
- Li Shenshi (李申時) - Li Tianyang and He Qixia's son. As a child, he was tutored in martial arts by Long Xiaoyun. He is captured by Wei Zhongxian's men during a skirmish, but his father releases him and his companions secretly and leaves with them. He succeeds in persuading his mother to reconcile with his father. After his marriage to He E'hua, he is accepted by Taoist Baishi as a student and studies Wudang swordplay for some time before eventually returning to Emei.

Mount Heaven Sect (天山派) and associates

- Huo Tiandu (霍天都) - Yue Mingke's teacher. He travels around the *jianghu* to learn various types of swordplay and develop new techniques to counter them. After years of study, he becomes a formidable swordsman and has created his own set of swordplay movements, which later becomes known as the "Mount Heaven Swordplay" (天山劍法).
- Ling Muhua (凌慕華) - Huo Tiandu's wife. She develops a rivalry with her husband to become the best sword fighter in the *jianghu* and leaves him and settles in a cave on Mount Hua. She creates a new set of sword techniques to counter her husband's. Once, she chances upon the baby Lian Nichang, adopts her and accepts her as a student. She dies when her inner energy flow goes haywire during a practice session that went wrong.
- Yang Yuncong (楊雲驄) - Yang Lian's young son. He is saved by Luo Tiebi when his father is imprisoned and murdered. Through Lian Nichang's recommendation, Luo brings the boy to Reverend Huiming. Huiming likes the child and accepts him as a disciple.
- Chu Zhaonan (楚昭南) - a boy from Hunan who travels to Xinjiang with his family to escape the chaos in Ming China. His parents commit suicide after their livestock is seized by Mengsasi's men. Huiming chances upon the boy and saves him and accepts him as a disciple.

Heaven Dragon Sect of Tibet (西藏天龍派)

- Tianlong Shangren (天龍上人) - leader of the sect. He possesses immense inner energy. At Fengsha Castle, he challenges Zhuo Yihang to a contest, in which Zhuo has to knock him down within three moves, while he will remain seated and not retaliate. Zhuo is unable to

defeat him initially, but Lian Nichang appears and throws a projectile at him when Zhuo is about to deliver the third blow, causing him to loose balance and fall off.
- Tiande Shangren (天德上人) - an elder of the sect. He serves the Kazakh tribe's chief as an advisor and abuses his authority by extorting from the common people. He attempts to force Xin Longzi to be his student, but Zhuo Yihang appears and drives him away. He is slain by Zhuo Yihang during the tribal chiefs' meeting.
- Leimeng (雷蒙) - Tianlong's oldest disciple. He is killed by Lian Nichang.
- Elder Wutou (烏頭長老) - an elder of the sect. He joins Huo Yuanzhong, Taoist Zhuo and Changqin to attack Lian Nichang, but is defeated and slain by Lian.

Zhuo family

- Zhuo Zhonglian (卓仲廉) - Zhuo Yihang's grandfather. He was formerly the governor of Yunnan and Guizhou. While on the way home after his retirement, he was captured by Lian Nichang's bandit gang and taken to their stronghold. Lian labelled him as "in between a honest and a corrupt government official", and took away a portion of his fortune (said to be ill-gotten gains) before releasing him. He dies from overwhelming grief after hearing news of the death of his son.
- Zhuo Jixian (卓繼賢) - Zhuo Zhonglian's son and Zhuo Yihang's father. He served in the Ministry of Revenue. He was implicated in the Case of the Palace Assault and executed on charges of treason without standing trial. His name is cleared when the truth behind the case is revealed.

Fengsha Castle (風砂堡)

- Cheng Zhangwu (成章五) - formerly a bandit chief from Huainan. He settles in Xinjiang and becomes the master of Fengsha Castle. He hires many expert pugilists to help him fight Lian Nichang and Zhuo Yihang, hoping that defeating them will make him famous.
- Cheng Zhangzhu (成掌珠) - Cheng Zhangwu's daughter. She is defeated by He Lühua in a duel.

Murong Chong and associates

- Murong Chong (慕容沖) - a highly-skilled Hui pugilist from Gansu. He specializes in fist styles of martial arts. He seeks fame and glory, and willingly joins the government service, becoming chief instructor of the Eastern Factory (東廠) guards. Despite working for Wei Zhongxian, he still maintains moral ethics, and decides to leave Wei after discovering that the latter is actually secretly conspiring with the Manchus. He engages Tie Feilong in a duel and saves Tie's life when Wei's men show up to interrupt them. He repents from his past misdeeds and roams the *jianghu*. He appears to help Zhuo Yihang escape from Wudang.
- Dingxu (定虛) - from the Kunlun Mountains. He taught Murong Chong the "72 Styles of Divine Fist".
- Jiao Manzi (焦蠻子) - a lone bandit from the northwest. He taught Murong Chong the "Eagle Claw" and "Iron Vest".

Tang clan

- Tang Jiabi (唐家壁) - Tang Qingchuan's son. His father sends him and Du Mingzhong to demand back two items that were robbed from them by Zhu Baochun.
- Tang Qingchuan (唐青川) - patriarch of the Tang clan. He specializes in using *anqi*.
- Du Mingzhong (杜明忠) - Tang Jiabi's escort

Chang'an Escort Agency (長安鏢局)

- Long Dasan (龍達三) - third master of the Chang'an Escort Agency. He is a friend of Liu Ximing. Tie Feilong saved him from some bandits before and he feels grateful to Tie. He helps Lian Nichang prepare some protective items for the duel with Gongsun Daniang.
- Lin Zhenjiao (林振蛟) - Long Dasan's deputy

Bandits

- "Twin Killers of Xichuan" (西川雙煞) - two brothers surnamed Peng (彭)
- Zhou Tong (周同) - nicknamed "Mountain Flipping Tiger" (翻山虎)
- Zhu Baozhuang (朱寶椿) - nicknamed "Fiery Spiritual Ape" (火靈猿)
- Fang brothers - from the Daba Mountains. They are killed by Lian Nichang.
- "Three Heroes of the Mai Family" (麥氏三雄) - three brothers who lead a bandit gang on Mount Dingjun
  - Mai Fengchun (麥逢春) - the oldest of the trio
- Tu Jingxiong (屠景雄) - leader of the Dragon Gate Gang (龍門幫)
- Shao Xuanyang (邵宣揚) - from southern Shanxi. He uses a smoking pipe as his weapon.
- Gui Youzhang (歸有章) - from eastern Sichuan, nicknamed "Eagle Claw King" (鷹爪王). He is killed by Lian Nichang.
- Maheizi (麻黑子) - a bandit leader from Kaifeng. He hires Jin Qianyan to help him after Tie Shanhu steals some of his loot. He is knocked down by Yue Mingke and rolls down a slope.
- Zhu Baochun (朱寶椿)
- Heaven-crossing Star (過天星)
- Nine Sections Fox (九節狸)

Others

- Taoist Zhenqian (貞乾道人) - a Taoist from Mount Hua. He is a close friend of the Five Elders of Wudang and Huo Tiandu. Yue Mingke passes him the swordplay manual left behind by Ling Muhua and asks him to bring it to his teacher. He is murdered by Jin Qianyan.

- Huo Yuanzhong (霍元仲) - a reputable martial artist from Shanxi. He attempts to kill Gongsun Lei's family together with Taoist Zhuo and Zhichan Shangren, but Tie Feilong and Lian Nichang manage to stop them in time. He joins Chanqin, Elder Wutou and Taoist Zhuo to confront the White Haired Demoness on Mount Heaven years later, but they are defeated by her.
- Taoist Zhuo (拙道人) - he and Zhichan Shangren are the surviving ones of the 13 pugilists who fought with Gongsun Daniang decades ago. They seek vengeance on her but she had already died so they attack Gongsun Lei and his family instead. They are defeated and driven away by Tie Feilong and Lian Nichang.
- Zhichan Shangren (智禪上人)
- Luo Tiebi (羅鐵臂) - a pugilist who saves the young Yang Yuncong when the boy's father (Yang Lian) is imprisoned by Wei Zhongxian. He brings Yang to Reverend Huiming through Lian Nichang's recommendation.
- Luo Jinfeng (羅金峰) - a pugilist from Jibei. He discovers that the Manchus are planning to send spies to infiltrate Ming China and manages to find out the identities of two of the spies. He passes on the secret to his friend, Meng Can, but is murdered by Ying Xiuyang.
- Qiu Taixu (邱太虛) - nicknamed "Sun and Moon Wheel" (日月輪)
- Lushi (盧師) - a monk who founded the Kunlu Sword Sect (昆盧劍派)
- Three Sang Devils (桑家三妖) - three villains who used to terrorize the Mount Heaven region. They are defeated and driven away by Lian Nichang.
  - Sangqian (桑乾)
  - Sanggua (桑弧)
  - Sangren (桑仁)

Source (edited): "http://en.wikipedia.org/wiki/List_of_Baifa_Mon%C3%BC_Zhuan_characters"

List of Qijian Xia Tianshan characters

The following is a list of characters from Liang Yusheng's *wuxia* novel *Qijian Xia Tianshan*. Some of these characters also appear in *Baifa Monü Zhuan* and *Saiwai Qixia Zhuan*.

Mount Heaven Sect (天山派)

- Ling Weifeng (凌未風) - nicknamed "Holy Light of Mount Heaven" (天山神芒) after his famous *anqi* (projectile weapon). Years ago, he was tricked into revealing the identities of the anti-Qing rebels. He attempted suicide in guilt after being slapped and accused by Liu Yufang, but refrained from doing so upon encountering the dying Yang Yuncong. He follows Yang's instructions and brings Yang's orphaned daughter to Reverend Huiming. He becomes Huiming's third disciple and emerges as a formidable swordsman years later. However, he has a strong tendency to suffer from seizures when exposed to the cold. This becomes his fatal weakness, as he experiences a sudden seizure during a fight with Chu Zhaonan, when he is just about to kill Chu. Chu turns the tables on him and captures him, imprisoning him in a labyrinth in Tibet. Chu also cuts off his right thumb, preventing him from using a sword again. He survives his ordeal and continues his heroic quest as a Mount Heaven swordsman dedicated to upholding justice and helping the poor.
- Yilan Zhu (易蘭珠) - Yang Yuncong and Nalan Minghui's daughter. She was brought to Mount Heaven by Ling Weifeng, and raised and tutored in martial arts by him and Reverend Huiming. She assassinates Prince Dodo to avenge her father, but is captured and imprisoned. She becomes Zhang Huazhao's love interest and marries him eventually.
- Chu Zhaonan (楚昭南) - the second student of Reverend Huiming. He inherits the Soaring Dragon Sword (游龍劍). He succumbs to temptations of fame and glory, and becomes a servant of Wu Sangui. He betrays Wu later and defects to serve the Kangxi Emperor, who appoints him as chief of the imperial guards. He is defeated by Yilan Zhu in the final battle in the Tibetan labyrinth and sustains serious injuries, including the loss of his left arm. He chooses to commit suicide to avoid humiliation.
- Yang Yuncong (楊雲驄) - the most senior student of Huiming. He inherits the Jade Breaking Sword (斷玉劍). He has a secret affair with Nalan Minghui, who bore him a daughter. However, he cannot be together with Nalan as she is forced to marry Prince Dodo. He is severely injured by Niuhuru and dies from his wounds after killing his foe. He entrusts his infant daughter to Ling Weifeng before his death.
- Reverend Huiming (晦明禪師) - a reclusive monk residing on Mount Heaven. He is considered a grandmaster of martial arts and one of the most powerful pugilists of his time. He dies in peace at the age of 112.
- Wuxing (悟性) - a monk who serves as Huiming's personal assistant

Gui Zhongming and associates

- Gui Zhongming (桂仲明) - son of Shi Tiancheng. He is adopted by Gui Tianlan and takes on his stepfather's surname. He is drawn into the conflict between his father and stepfather, and goes berserk after thinking that he had killed his father in his rage. He loses memory of his past and starts sleepwalking, during which he attacks people without knowing. He meets Mao Wanlian and Fu Qingzhu, who help to cure

him of his mental illness and reunite him with his family. He falls in love with Mao and becomes extremely protective of her. Despite his formidable prowess in swordplay and *anqi*, he is reckless, nonchalant, easily agitated, and bereft of social etiquette. He becomes the founder of the northern branch of the Wudang Sect.
- Gui Tianlan (桂天瀾) - the senior student of Ye Yunsun. He brings Shi Tiancheng's family with him to join Zhang Xianzhong's forces, and settles at Jiange after Sichuan falls to the Qing army. Believing that Shi Tiancheng had died, he marries Shi's wife and adopts Shi's children. He is killed in a fight against Shi and four imperial guards.
- Shi Daniang (石大娘) - Ye Yunsun's daughter. She marries Shi Tiancheng and bears him Zhongming and Zhujun. After her husband's apparent death, she marries Gui Tianlan, who helps to take care of her and her children. She and Gui maintain a sibling-like relationship even though they are a married couple in name. She is well-versed in the "Five Birds Swordplay" (五禽劍法) and imparts this skill to her son.
- Shi Zhujun (石竹君) - Gui Zhongming's younger sister
- Ye Yunsun (葉雲蓀) - Gui Zhongming's maternal grandfather. He treated Gui Tianlan and Shi Tiancheng like his sons and tutored them in martial arts.
- Yu Zhong (于中) - Shi Tiancheng's student. He saved his teacher when the latter attempted suicide by leaping off a cliff.

Zhongnan Sect (終南派) and associates

- Fu Qingzhu (傅青主) - a eccentric master swordsman and physician. He is renowned for his mastery of the "Wuji Swordplay" (無極劍法).
- Mao Wanlian (冒浣蓮) - Mao Pijiang and Dong Xiaowan's daughter. She was raised and tutored in martial arts by Fu Qingzhu. She meets Gui Zhongming, who was suffering from hallucinations then, and helps him recover from his mental illness and reunite him with his family. Gui falls in love with her and becomes extremely protective of her. Just like her parents, she is talented in poetry and literary arts. She develops a close relationship with Nalan Rongruo because of their common interest. She marries Gui Zhongming eventually.
- Shan Sinan (單思南) - Fu Qingzhu's senior and Liu Jingyi's close friend. He becomes Liu Yufang's godfather and mentors her in swordplay.

Wu family

- Wu Yuanying (武元英) - master of the Wu Family Manor and a close friend of Fu Qingzhu. He offers shelter to the rebels in his residence.
- Wu Chenghua (武成化) - Wu Yuanying's son

White Haired Demoness and associates

- White Haired Demoness (白髮魔女) - lover of Zhuo Yihang in *Baifa Monü Zhuan*. She was heartbroken after misbelieving that Zhuo had betrayed her love and her hair turned white overnight. She dies at the age of 100, and her corpse is last seen lying beside the shrunken remains of Zhuo Yihang.
- Hamaya (哈瑪雅) - nicknamed "Flying Red Sash" (飛紅巾). She is a disciple of the White Haired Demoness and a former love rival of Nalan Minghui in *Saiwai Qixia Zhuan*. Her hair turned white overnight after Yang Yuncong rejected her. She resolves her rivalry with Nalan and saves Yilan Zhu from death. She transfers her love for Yang Yuncong to Yilan Zhu and treats the latter like her daughter. She returns to her former position as leader of the tribal people of Xinjiang at the end of the novel.
- Wu Qiongyao (武瓊瑤) - Wu Yuanying's daughter. By chance, she encounters the White Haired Demoness, who likes her and accepts her as a disciple. Despite studying martial arts only for three years under the Demoness' tutelage, she emerges as a powerful swordswoman. She marries Li Siyong eventually and bears him a son and a daughter. She settles on Mount Heaven with her children after her husband's death.

Wudang Sect (武當派)

- Xin Longzi (辛龍子) - the first disciple of Zhuo Yihang. Even though he started learning from Zhuo before Shi Tiancheng, he is younger than Shi, hence his teacher wanted him to address Shi as his senior. While in Tibet once, he saw Han Zhibang practicing martial arts from the *Sinew-changing Classic*, and immediately realized that the manual contained the missing moves to his teacher's "Bodhidharma Swordplay". He seizes the manual from Han through trickery and masters the skills within it, becoming even more powerful than before. He desires to possess a precious sword of his own and is tricked by Chu Zhaonan into helping the villains. Chu attempts to kill him to seize his manual but he survives and is saved by Ling Weifeng. He is turned back to the path of goodness by Ling and decides to follow his benefactor. He engages Qi Zhenjun in a prolonged duel and inflicts the killing blow on Qi after the latter is severely injured by Shi Tiancheng. However, he suffers from over exhaustion and dies shortly after the fight.
- Shi Tiancheng (石天成) - Gui Tianlan's junior. He leaves to fetch his relatives during the Qing invasion of Sichuan and entrusts his family to Gui Tianlan's care. He is thought to be dead, so Gui marries his wife and adopts his children. When he returns later, he thought that Gui had betrayed him by taking away his family from him. He is accepted by Zhuo Yihang as a disciple, despite already having a background in other forms of martial

arts. He returns to confront Gui later and causes the latter to die. He regrets upon learning the truth from his wife after Gui's death. He promises that the firstborn child of his son shall bear Gui's surname, as a form of compensation to his late senior. He helps Xin Longzi in the fight against Qi Zhenjun, managing to inflict severe wounds on Qi. However, he is also mortally wounded and dies from his injuries later.

- Zhuo Yihang (卓一航) - lover of the White Haired Demoness and former leader of the Wudang Sect in *Baifa Monü Zhuan*. He is already dead when the events of the novel take place. He finally obtains the flowers that can turn his lover's white hair black again, but does not live to pass them to her personally. Before his death, he tells Xin Longzi to use chemical means to reduce the size of his body, in order to prevent his enemies from identifying and destroying his remains. His skeleton is last seen lying beside the corpse of the White Haired Demoness.
- Xuanzhen (玄貞) - a disciple of Taoist Huangye and current leader of the Wudang Sect. He encounters Wu Qiongyao and duels with her when she teases him about his skills. He is unable to defeat Wu and feels angry and ashamed. At the end of the novel, he gives up his position as leader of Wudang to Gui Zhongming after seeing that Gui had mastered their sect's long-lost "Bodhidharma Swordplay".
- He Lühua (何綠華) - a character from *Baifa Monü Zhuan*. Although she is nearing the age of 50 in the novel's setting, she is described to be still looking youthful. She accompanies Xuanzhen on the journey to Xinjiang.
- He Lühua's husband - his name is not mentioned in the novel. He accompanies his wife and Xuanzhen to Xinjiang.
- Xuanzhen's juniors - they accompany Xuanzhen to Xinjiang
  - Xuantong (玄通)
  - Xuanjue (玄覺)

Heaven and Earth Society (天地會)

- Han Zhibang (韓志邦) - initially a stable keeper, he became the leader of the anti-Qing Heaven and Earth Society. He passes the leadership position to Liu Yufang later. He has a secret crush on Liu, but does not dare to admit it and decides to leave after seeing that she has affections for Ling Weifeng. He finds the *Sinew-changing Classic* and masters an incomplete set of the skills, which temporarily boosts his prowess in martial arts. He helps the lamas retrieve the stolen śarīras and earns their respect in return. He uses his close relations with the Tibetans to help the rebels on a few occasions. He encounters the dying Xin Longzi later and obliges to Xin's final request to join the Wudang Sect. He receives back the *Sinew-changing Classic* and passes his knowledge of the "Bodhidharma Swordplay" to Gui Zhongming later. He willingly sacrifices himself to save Ling Weifeng, by secretly switching places with Ling. He attempts to ambush Chu Zhaonan when the latter comes to check on Ling Weifeng, but is no match for Chu and dies under Chu's sword.
- Yang Yiwei (楊一維)
- Hua Zishan (華紫山)

Southern Ming rebels

- Liu Yufang (劉郁芳) - Liu Jingyi's daughter, nicknamed "Brocade Cloud Sword" (雲錦劍). She leads the rebels to resist Dodo's forces in Hangzhou. She succeeds Han Zhibang as leader of the Heaven and Earth Society later. She becomes a "Friend of Mount Heaven" (an ally of the Seven Swords) at the end of the novel.
- Zhang Huazhao (張華昭) - son of Zhang Huangyan. He attempts to assassinate Dodo on Mount Wutai but fails due to Yilan Zhu's untimely interruption. He falls in love with Yilan Zhu and goes through troubles to save her from death. In addition to his reunion with Yilan Zhu after she is rescued by Hamaya, he also learns a set of *qinggong* techniques from the White Haired Demoness. He marries Yilan Zhu at the end of the novel, and also joins the Wudang Sect as Gui Zhongming's junior, becoming a master in the "Bodhidharma Swordplay".
- Monk Tongming (通明和尚) - nicknamed "Strange Monk" (怪頭陀)
- Chang Ying (常英) - nicknamed "God of Death" (喪門神)
- Cheng Tong (程通) - nicknamed "Iron Tower" (鐵塔)
- Prince Lu (魯王) - a self-appointed Regent (監國) of the Southern Ming Dynasty
- Prince Lu's followers
  - Zhang Huangyan (張煌言)
  - Zhang Mingzhen (張名振)
  - Liu Jingyi (劉精一)

Mount Changbai Sect (長白山派)

- Qi Zhenjun (齊真君) - founder of the sect. In his younger days, he challenged Reverend Huiming to a duel but was refused by the latter, leading him to falsely believe that he was better than Huiming. He encountered the White Haired Demoness later and was defeated by her and driven away. He spent the next 50 years improving his skills in the Changbai Mountains and becomes a formidable swordsman. He returns to assist the Qing government in dealing with the rebels. He is severely injured by Shi Tiancheng in a fight and is eventually slain by Xin Longzi.
- Qiu Dongluo (邱東洛) - Niuhuru's junior. He wields a saber and a sword in combat and uses a variety of combination attacks to confuse his opponents. He uses on a fake Han Chinese identity to gather news in the *jianghu*. He is responsible for disfiguring Ling Weifeng when the latter was bringing the baby Yilan Zhu to Mount Heaven. He encounters Ling again several years later and had his ears sliced off by

Ling for revenge. He is killed by Yilan Zhu in a later fight.
- Niuhuru (紐祜盧) - a Manchu martial artist and disciple of Qi Zhenjun. He is slain by Yang Yuncong in a fight but manages to injure Yang mortally before dying.
- Liu Xiyan (柳西岩) - a disciple of Qi Zhenjun. He follows his teacher and Qiu Dongluo to help the Qing government fight the rebels.

Qing Dynasty

Royal family

- Shunzhi Emperor (順治皇帝) - the former ruler of the Qing Empire. He retired from state affairs and became a monk to seek redemption after the death of Dong Xiaowan. He leads a reclusive life in Qingliang Monastery on Mount Wutai. He is murdered by Yan Zhongtian on his son's orders.
- Kangxi Emperor (康熙皇帝) - the son of Shunzhi and present ruler of the Qing Empire. He orders Yan Zhongtian to murder his father, and attempts to silence Yan as well by poisoning him.
- Third Princess (三公主) - the third daughter of Shunzhi and sister of Kangxi. She often sneaks out to find Nalan Rongruo to escape the boredom of being confined in the palace. Once, Nalan requested a special medicine from her to heal the injured Zhang Huazhao, and she insisted on meeting Nalan's new guest. She becomes attracted to Zhang and develops a crush on him. She decides to sacrifice herself to help Zhang rescue Yilan Zhu, because she knows Zhang truly loves Yilan Zhu. She commits suicide after stealing a special imperial seal from Kangxi that can authorize Yilan Zhu's release from prison.

Nobles

- Dodo, Prince Yu (豫親王 多鐸) - a Manchu noble who serves as governor of Jiangnan and Jiangxi. He is well versed in military strategy and martial arts. He loves Nalan Minghui even though he is aware that she is unhappy about their forced marriage. He is assassinated by Yilan Zhu, and dies in his wife's arms.
- Nalan Minghui (納蘭明慧) - Nalan Xiuji's daughter. She is talented in both literary and martial arts. She had a secret love affair with Yang Yuncong and bore him a daughter, but is forced to marry Dodo. Even though she treats Dodo indifferently after their marriage, she still respects him as her husband. When Yilan Zhu returns to take revenge on Dodo, she tries to stop both sides from harming each other but fails. When Yilan Zhu is imprisoned for murdering Dodo, she tries to save her daughter but is unable to do so and she commits suicide.
- Nalan Xingde (納蘭性德) - referred to as "Nalan Rongruo" (納蘭容若) in the novel. He is Yilan Zhu's cousin. He is talented in literary arts. His reputation as a renowned scholar and poet earns him the favour of Kangxi. He has a strong disdain for bloodshed and conflict, and constantly hopes that everyone in the Qing Empire can live in harmony. He secretly helps the rebels on numerous occasions.
- Nalan Mingzhu (納蘭明珠) - Nalan Rongruo's father. He pretends to be a patron of literary arts by hiring people to help him write poems and pieces of literature, so as to win the favour of Kangxi, who likes intellectuals and literati. His son, in contrast with him, is the one who truly appreciates the arts.
- Nalan Xiuji (納蘭秀吉) - a Manchu general who contributed to the founding of the Qing Dynasty. He is appointed as chief of Hangzhou's military forces.
- Yunti (允禵) - the 14th son of Kangxi. He leads the Qing army to conquer Tibet and capture the Dalai Lama.
- Geji, Prince Cheng (成親王 格濟) - a Manchu noble in command of the Qing army attacking Xinjiang. He is well versed in military strategy but is not good in martial arts.

Generals, governors and officials

- Chen Jin (陳錦) - one of Dodo's generals. He conquered Prince Lu's Southern Ming regime.
- Hutu Nuke (呼圖努克) - a Qing general leading the attack on Xinjiang
- Zhao Liangdong (趙良棟) - governor-general of Sichuan and Shaanxi
- Li Benshen (李本深) - West Pacifying General of Kunming
- Zhu Guozhi (朱國治) - Inspector of Yunnan
- Hong Chengchou (洪承疇)

Imperial guards (禁衛軍)

- Zhang Chengbin (張承斌) - second-in-command of the imperial guards. Dodo orders him to lead 3,000 men on a manhunt for the rebels, and he arrives at the Wu Family Manor. He is ordered to retreat by Yan Zhongtian, who is superior in rank to him.
- Hu Tianzhu (胡天柱) - an imperial guard commander ranking below Chu Zhaonan and Zhang Chengbin. He follows Chu to capture Gui Zhongming and the other rebels hiding in Nalan Rongruo's house. He is defeated by Meng Wuwei and knocked into a ditch.
- Gu Yuanliang (古元亮) - an imperial guard from Henan who specializes in *dianxue* techniques. He follows Chu Zhaonan to seize the śarīras.
- Hao Dashou (郝大綬) - an imperial guard who follows Chu Zhaonan to seize the śarīras. He is killed by the Tibetan lamas protecting the relics.
- Zhang Kui (張魁) - he, Peng Kunlin and Hao Jiming follow Qiu Dongluo to hunt down and kill Ling Weifeng. He uses a red copper saber. He has his arm sliced off by Liu Yufang in a fight.
- Peng Kunlin (彭昆林) - uses a white wax pole
- Hao Jiming (郝繼明) - uses a pair of grappling hooks. He is the most powerful of the three.

- Jiao Ba (焦霸) - a former bandit nicknamed "Eight-armed Nezha" (八臂哪吒). He and three other guards are sent to hunt down and kill Gui Tianlan. He is killed by Shi Tiancheng, who grabs him and they fall off a cliff together.
- Wang Gang (王剛) - specializes in "Vajra Sanshou" (金剛散手). He wants to become chief of the imperial guards but is disappointed when Chu Zhaonan takes the position. He intends to defeat and capture Ling Weifeng to prove his ability but fails. After his defeat, he grabs Mao Wanlian and holds her hostage, but Ling saves Mao and kills him with his *anqi*.
- Shen Tianbao (申天豹) - he and his brother are students of Hong Sibazi (洪四把子), a martial arts master from Cangzhou. They are skilled in the "Wugou Swordplay" (吳鉤劍法). They are slain by Ling Weifeng in a duel.
- Shen Tianhu (申天虎) - Shen Tianbao's brother.
- Diao Sifu (刁四福) - an imperial guard serving under Chu Zhaonan. He is good in *qinggong* and slightly better than Han Zhibang in martial arts.

Palace guards (大內侍衛)

- Cheng Tianting (成天挺) - a palace guard commander nicknamed "Iron Brush Judge" (鐵筆判官). He specializes in *dianxue* techniques and uses a pair of ink brushes in combat. He is almost on par with Chu Zhaonan in terms of martial arts. At the end of the novel, he is caught off guard and immobilized by Han Zhibang while watching over the captive Ling Weifeng. He is defeated and slain by the combined efforts of Yilan Zhu and Liu Yufang.
- Yan Zhongtian (閻中天) - a trusted bodyguard of Kangxi. He discovers that Shunzhi is still alive and has become a monk. Kangxi forces him to murder Shunzhi and attempts to poison him to death later to silence him. He is saved by Ling Weifeng and given medical treatment by Fu Qingzhu. He sacrifices himself to help the rebels call off Zhang Chengbin's troops, and dies from poisoning as his healing process was interrupted.
- Zheng Tiepai (鄭鐵牌) - a palace guard who uses a pair of iron shields in combat. He is slain by Ling Weifeng.
- Cheng Tianting's deputies
  - Zheng Dakun (鄭大錕)
  - Lian Sanhu (連三虎) - blinded by Wu Qiongyao in a fight

Others

- Hong Tao (洪濤) - he and Jiao Zhi are guards from the residence of the governor-general of Sichuan and Shaanxi. They lead Wang Gang and the Shen brothers to Gui Tianlan's house. They are slain by Gui Zhongming in a duel.
- Jiao Zhi (焦直)
- Lu Ming (陸明) - a martial arts instructor in Nalan Mingzhu's residence.
- Lu Liang (陸亮) - Lu Ming's brother.
- Zhou Qing (周青) - one of the guards watching over Ling Weifeng when the latter is imprisoned in the labyrinth. His grandfather served Dorgon during Shunzhi's reign and was killed after helping his master complete a secret mission. Ling enlightens him about true friendship and loyalty. He is impressed with Ling and befriends him, secretly agreeing to help Ling escape.
- Ma Fang (馬方) - Zhou Qing's colleague. He is a native of Xinjiang and was recommended by Shang Yunting to serve the Qing court. He is ashamed of himself when Ling tells him about how Qing soldiers invade his homeland and mistreat his people. Like many others, he becomes impressed with Ling and decides to help Ling escape.

Li Laiheng forces

- Li Siyong (李思永) - Li Laiheng's younger brother. He is well versed in both military and literary arts, and specializes in using *anqi* (暗器). He is sent as an envoy to discuss a truce and temporary alliance with Wu Sangui. He marries Wu Qiongyao, whom he met and fell in love with in Xinjiang. At the end of the novel, he is killed in action in western Sichuan.
- Li Laiheng (李來亨) - foster son of Li Jin. He escapes to Yunnan with Li Zicheng's remnant forces and forms an insurgent army to resist the Qing Dynasty. He commits suicide after his army is defeated and besieged by Qing forces.
- Li Jin (李錦) - nephew of Li Zicheng. He is killed in action in Henan against Qing forces.
- Zhang Qingyuan (張清原) - sent by Li Laiheng to lead a group of men to eliminate the Five Dragons Gang.
- Jiang Zhuang (蔣壯) - Zhang Qingyuan's deputy. He is injured by Zhang Yihu and healed by Fu Qingzhu later.

Bandits

The following pugilists initially plotted with Han Jing to rob Li Dingguo's treasure. They are impressed with Ling Weifeng's heroism and skills after losing to him in a contest, and agree to submit to him. Ling recommends them to join Li Laiheng's rebel force later.

- Zhang Yuanzhen (張元振) - nicknamed "Eight Directions Saber" (八方刀).
- Tao Hong (陶宏) - nicknamed "Dark Fearsome Deity" (黑煞神). He specializes in wrestling.
- Luo Da (羅達) - a bandit chief from Mount Mei in northern Sichuan. He is the most greedy of the group, and was the first to charge into the treasure cave. He is injured by the traps.
- Da Sangong (達三公) - the headman of a tribe. He is referred to as "Headman Da" (達土司) in the novel. He specializes in the "Iron Vest Skill" (鐵布衫), which allows him to concentrate inner energy on parts of his body and make them extremely tough and impenetrable by sharp weapons.
- Lu Dalengzi (盧大楞子) - chief of the Qingyang Gang (青陽幫). He is

the most honest and lawful of the group. He loses to Ling Weifeng in a *qinggong* competition.

Li Dingguo forces

- Li Dingguo (李定國) - former deputy of Zhang Xianzhong. He took control of Sichuan after Zhang's death and resisted the Qing invaders until his death. He left behind a treasure hoard for future generations intending to continue his legacy. The treasure comprises eighteen giant statues of himself, all made of gold. He also left behind a precious Soaring Dragon Sword (騰蛟劍), which once belonged to Xiong Ting-bi. The sword becomes Gui Zhongming's weapon.
- Han Jing (韓荊) - former subordinate of Li Dingguo. He is a hunchback, and specializes in the "Heavenly Demon Staff Skill" (天魔杖法). He loses to Ling Weifeng in a contest of inner energy and pledges allegiance to Ling later. Ling suggests to him to bring his fellows to join Li Laiheng's rebel force.
- He Wanfang (賀萬方) - a craftsman who worked with Gui Tianlan on constructing the traps in the treasure cave. He leads Han Jing and company into the cave to rob the treasure. He follows the others to join Li Laiheng later.
- Zhu Tianmu (朱天木) - killed in action against Qing forces
- Yang Qingbo (楊青波) - killed in action against Qing forces

Wuwei Escort Agency (武威鏢局)

- Meng Wuwei (孟武威) - master of the agency. He has a strong reputation in the *jianghu* and most bandits would usually avoid robbing his convoys. He uses a tobacco pipe to blow smoke patterns whenever his men are escorting a convoy, so as to alert potential robbers to his presence. He also uses the pipe as a *dianxue* weapon. He and his son appear to help the protagonists fight Chu Zhaonan and some imperial guards at one point.
- Meng Jian (孟堅) - Meng Wuwei's son. He is tasked with escorting a group of maidens to Nalan Mingzhu's residence, with the Lu brothers assisting him. He runs into the Three Devils, who attempt to seize the maidens from him. He is no match for them and manages to survive when Gui Zhongming and Mao Wanlian appear to help him.

Tibet

- Dalai Lama (達賴活佛)
- Red robed lama (紅衣喇嘛) - sent by the Dalai Lama to follow Chu Zhaonan to meet Wu Sangui and affirm their alliance. He discovers that Chu is planning to betray Wu. Chu attempts to kill him to silence him. He is saved by Ling Weifeng and brings news of Wu's rebellion to the Southern Ming rebels. He is killed by Chu Zhaonan during the battle in the Tibetan labyrinth near the end of the novel.
- Zongda Wanzhen (宗達完真) - one of the lamas escorting the śarīras. He is instated as the Dalai Lama by Yunti when Qing forces occupied Tibet. He agrees to help Han Zhibang save Ling Weifeng from prison and is so impressed with Han's sacrifice that he called Han a *tulku*.

Heaven Dragon Sect (天龍派)

- Tianlong Shangren (天龍上人) - leader and founder of the sect
- Tianmeng Shangren (天蒙上人) - Tianlong's junior
- Tianxiong Shangren (天雄上人) - another junior of Tianlong. He and Qi Zhenjun appear at the tribal chiefs' meeting to help Menglu "persuade" the chiefs into submitting to the Qing government. He is defeated by Xin Longzi in a fight.

Tribal people of Xinjiang

- Maigaiti (麥蓋提) - a close friend of Yang Yuncong in *Saiwai Qixia Zhuan*
- Manlingna (曼鈴娜) - the wife of Maigaiti
- Yishida (伊士達) - a close friend of Yang Yuncong in *Saiwai Qixia Zhuan*. He attempts to stop Menglu from persuading the tribal people to surrender to the Qing government. Menglu attacks him and he dies from his injuries later. He passes the guardian sword of the Heaven Dragon Sect (previously obtained by Yang Yuncong) to Ling Weifeng, who passes it to Xin Longzi later.
- Menglu (孟祿) - chief of the Keda'er (喀達爾) tribe. In *Saiwai Qixia Zhuan*, he once accused Yang Yuncong of being a spy when Yang started a romance with Nalan Minghui. He allies with the Qing government and attempts to persuade the tribes in Xinjiang to submit to Qing. His plan is disrupted by his daughter and Hukeji.
- Mengmanlisi (孟曼麗絲) - Menglu's daughter. She is aware that her father is "selling out" their people by helping the Qing government. She disrupts his plan with the help of Hukeji, who is in love with her.
- Hukeji (呼克濟) - the young chief of the Kazakh tribe. With help from Ling Weifeng and Xin Longzi, he succeeds in stopping Menglu from persuading the people to submit to the Qing government.
- Mengshan (孟山) - Menglu's son

Five Dragons Gang (五龍幫)

- Zhang Yihu (張一虎) - specializes in the "Iron Gravel Palm" (鐵沙掌). He is captured by Fu Qingzhu and commits suicide.
- Li Erbao (李二豹) - specializes in using the three-section staff. He is killed by Gui Zhongming.
- Zhao Sanqi (趙三麒) - specializes in the "Earth Kick" (地堂腿). He is killed by Fu Qingzhu.
- Qian Silin (錢四麟) - specializes in the "Five Elements Fist" (五行拳). He is killed by Gui Zhongming.
- Tang Wuxiong (唐五熊) - specializes in *anqi*. He is killed by Fu Qingzhu.
- Ge Zhonglong (葛中龍) - a deceased martial artist from Yunnan. He taught each of the five gang leaders one of his five martial arts specialties.

Three Feudatories

Wu Sangui forces

- Wu Sangui (吳三桂) - the "West Suppressing Prince" (平西王) in charge of Yunnan and Sichuan. He plots a rebellion against the Qing Empire.
- Zhang Tianmeng (張天蒙) - Wu Sangui's subordinate. He steals the śarīras when Chu Zhaonan attempts to rob them from him. He is injured by Ling Weifeng and recuperates in a cave after escaping. He encounters Han Zhibang and is killed by Han in the ensuing fight.
- Fan Zheng (范錚) - one of the three best warriors serving under Wu Sangui (the other two being Chu Zhaonan and Zhang Tianmeng). He is skilled in using the "Sky-touching Swordplay" (摩雲劍). He is defeated by a bare-handed Ling Weifeng in a duel.
- Bao Zhu (保柱) - a general serving under Wu Sangui
- Wu Shifan (吳世璠) - Wu Sangui's grandson and successor

Shang Kexi forces

- Shang Kexi (尚可喜) - the "South Suppressing Prince" (平南王) in charge of Guangdong
- Shang Zhixin (尚之信) - Shang Kexi's son
- Jin Ya (金崖) - Shang Kexi's envoy to Wu Sangui

Geng Zhongming forces

- Geng Zhongming (耿仲明) - the "South Pacifying Prince" (靖南王) in charge of Fujian
- Geng Jingzhong (耿精忠) - Geng Zhongming's grandson

Others

- Shi Zhenfei (石振飛) - an elderly escort agency master and a close ally of the Heaven and Earth Society. Despite his age, he has a strong inner energy foundation, and is still capable of performing swordplay swiftly and accurately.
- Shang Yunting (尚雲亭) - leader of the Iron Fan Sect (鐵扇幫). He is initially reluctant to accept Hao Feifeng as his student, but falls for the latter's feminine charms and eventually agrees. He is defeated by Meng Wuwei and Shi Zhenfei, and driven away from Jiangnan. He arrives in Xinjiang and allies with Chu Zhaonan to counter the rebels, injuring Wu Yuanying in an unprovoked attack. He is defeated and captured by Fu Qingzhu and commits suicide in humiliation.
- Three Devils (三魔)
  - Hao Feifeng (郝飛鳳) - a *jianghu* lowlife and bandit. He behaves in a feminine manner and is seen as a transexual by his contemporaries. He and his companions attempt to seize the women escorted by Meng Jian. He uses an iron fan in combat. He follows his teacher to Xinjiang after their defeat by Meng Wuwei and Shi Zhenfei. He is captured after attempting to attack the Wu family, and is killed by Wu Qiongyao.
  - Sha Wuding (沙無定) - killed by Gui Zhongming
  - Liu Daxiong (柳大雄)
- Three Sang Devils (桑家三妖) - three villains who used to terrorize the Mount Heaven region, but were defeated and driven away by the White Haired Demoness. They return to Mount Heaven to seek vengeance several years later. They are defeated and slain by Ling Weifeng eventually.
  - Sangqian (桑乾)
  - Sanggua (桑弧)
  - Sangren (桑仁)
- Mao Xiang (冒襄) - referred to as "Mao Pijiang" (冒辟疆) in the novel. He is a famous scholar and patron of the arts, and a close friend of Fu Qingzhu. He died from anguish and frustration after losing his wife.
- Dong Xiaowan (董小宛) - a courtesan who married Mao Xiang because of their common interest in the arts. She was forcefully separated from her husband and brought to the palace to be Shunzhi's concubine. Shunzhi treated her well but the nobles despised her because she was a Han Chinese. She was killed on the empress dowager's orders.
- Wu Meicun (吳梅村) - a poet and scholar favoured by Shunzhi. He is secretly murdered on Kangxi's orders after writing a poem hinting that Shunzhi is still alive on Mount Wutai.
- Gu Liangfen (顧梁汾) - a close friend of Nalan Rongruo. When Wu Hancha was sent into exile, he wrote the *Jinlüqu* (金縷曲) to Nalan, hinting that he needed Nalan's help to save Wu. Mao Wanlian sang the song to Nalan when she needed his help in saving Ling Weifeng from Chu Zhaonan's clutches.
- Wu Hancha (吳漢槎) - a close friend of Nalan Rongruo. He was sent into exile but was saved from his fate by Nalan.

Source (edited): "http://en.wikipedia.org/wiki/List_of_Qijian_Xia_Tianshan_characters"